A LONG WAY
FROM
HOME 2
NATIONAL BEST SELLING AUTHOR
NIKI JILVONTAE

A Long Way From Home 2
-A Novel Written By-
Niki Jilvontae

Copyright © 2022 by Niki Jilvontae
Published by Niki Jilvontae

Facebook: Niki Jilvontae

Cover Design: Tina Shivers
Editor: Tamyra L. Griffin

Table of Contents

Rage filled my body as I listened intently to the news reporter talk about another missing girl. Eight years had passed since Justin and I escaped from the clutches of the devil, but all of my emotional scars were still fresh. I could still feel the chains tightly wrapped around my arms and hear the screams of terror ringing in my ears. Everything I had gone through was fresh on my mind, although I had hid it from the world.

I had focused on finishing school and becoming a well-known criminal psychologist in Los Angeles. I learned everything that I could about the criminal mind and began secretly building my own criminal profile on Abaddon, Tony, and Mark. The police hadn't been able to find any of them, but I was determined to get my revenge against them and stop them from hurting any more children. I felt my desire to kill them grow every time that I looked into my daughter's beautiful face. She was my everything, so innocent and kind. She was the total opposite of everything Abaddon was.

Justin and I were the best parents we could be to our daughter, always involved and attentive to her every need. We protected her like she was the Hope diamond from the time she came into the world. Now she has grown into a miniature version of myself, and we had the perfect storybook life. Justin was an up-and-coming architect with his own company, and we were doing great financially. To the world we seemed to have it all and be a prime example of people overcoming tragedy and persevering against all odds. However, we both still secretly struggled with our demons.

Justin got through by submerging himself in work and spending time with me and A'Miracle. However, I still often caught him sitting in the dark alone, still, and quiet. I knew it was those times he was reliving our days in hell, but he always quickly snapped out of it. He was still so strong, so rational. I, on the other hand, would have fits of rage when I was alone and left to think about all of the horrible things I saw and had to endure. My rage would consume me, and I would go over plans to kill pedophiles in my head. To relieve some of my anger and anxiety, I started taking self-defense classes and quickly became good at hand-to-hand combat. I was secretly preparing myself for what I felt I had to do. I had to find Abaddon. I knew that I could never rest or truly be happy until he was dead. I had to ensure A'Miracle would be safe, and Abaddon would not be able to hurt anyone else.

As I tried to calm myself by changing the channel, an Amber Alert on one of the news stations caught my eye. Fifteen-year-old Mikayla Johnson was missing from a park close to the subdivision by my home. Her friends stated to the police that she had been having problems with her family about her new, long-distance boyfriend. She decided to meet him in the park the night of her best friend's party, so that they would be nearby. The best friend and other party goers said they saw her talking to a tall, handsome, twenty something white guy by the entrance of the park. However, when they looked again they were gone. The friends later found her purse and all of its contents in a garbage can next to the entrance.

I don't know why, but I suddenly had the feeling that Abaddon had her. Rage started to consume me as I stood up and began pacing the floor. I was so happy Justin had taken A'Miracle to her playdate like he did every Saturday, because before I knew it I was cursing and searching for a rental car company on my laptop. I booked a car for the next Saturday and started preparing for my trip. I didn't know exactly what I'd do when I got to Vegas, but I knew I had to do something. I went into the basement and opened my secret trunk with the key I kept in the bottom of my jewelry box, revealing an arsenal of weapons. I mindlessly packed so many weapons in my bag a person would have thought I was preparing for war.

My hands shook as I put the manila envelope that held my criminal profiles into my bag. This would be the beginning of my revenge. I would seek out Tony and Mark - and make them pay for what they did. I would make them feel the torture I felt every night locked in that hell. Then I would show Abaddon that I could be just as coldhearted and menacing as he could. I would hunt him down like a dog and eradicate him. My living nightmare was over. No longer would those old demons haunt me. I would kill them all. It was my time to cause them all an amount of pain they never imagined. It was my time for Sweet Revenge!

"Seventy-one, seventy-two, seventy-three, Seventy- four.." I counted off as I did sit-ups on the basement floor while staring at the raggedy, dingy, pink- and-black stripper body suit with matching booty shorts that I had on when Quintika, Justin, Maria, and I escaped hell. I kept it hanging on the wall in the basement, hidden from Justin and A'Miracle as a reminder of the torture we went through. I didn't want to forget the terror and pain Abaddon had caused us. I needed that hate and anger to fuel my plan for revenge. I needed to relive that hell so that I would never forget the things he did or the friends we lost in that pit or turmoil. However, I could never forget Quintika, Tommy, Dontae, Cassie, Julie, and the others. I couldn't help but to remember them all and I vowed that someday I would make Abaddon feel pain ten times worse than he ever made us feel. The things that he did to Justin, Tommy, Quintitka, and I were forever imprinted in my memory and in my heart. I couldn't help but to see his cold, dark eyes every time that I was alone. It was like I could still feel his cold, clammy hands all over me and smell his hot, cigarette breath on my face.

"You're Abaddon's special girl.", echoed in my ears as I tried to drown out the sound of his voice by continuing my exercises harder and faster.

"Ninety, ninety-one, ninety-two.." I continued to count as my mind wandered back to the past.

I closed my eyes tight and continued to do sit-ups as my memories took me back to that room in hell where Abaddon took a part of me and replaced it with a part of him. Suddenly, I could hear the classical music fill my ears once again. I could feel the cool air on my face and smooth, cool floor beneath my feet. For a second I felt as if I were really back there again, dancing for my life as a madman stalked me like prey. I could feel his evil, lustful eyes roaming up and down my body as he stood back and watched me dance. Then just when my beautiful dance had me feeling as free as I had ever felt his arms were around me, pulling me to him and into his sadistic fantasy.

My trip down memory lane was so real in that moment I didn't even realize I had gotten up and was dancing across the basement floor with my eyes closed until I felt the cool concrete floor underneath my feet. I *plied* and then did a *developpe* in fast circles, holding my arms out to my side. I spent so fast and so gracefully, I felt as if I was a bird, and I would take flight at any second. I didn't know it, but my love for dance could still make me feel peaceful and free. I hadn't danced like that since we escaped our hell. However, in that moment I felt like not a second had passed as I continued to float all over the basement floor. Tears fell from my eyes and flew in the air as I continued to spin and dance until I felt as if my heart would burst. Suddenly the sound of applause startled me out of my haze, and I opened my tear-filled eyes to see my beautiful daughter and husband standing at the bottom of the basement steps. The Look on Justin's face told me that he saw my thoughts and he knew that I wasn't really right there in front of him. He knew that I was back in New York in that place, dancing for the devil.

I quickly shook off the heavy feeling in my heart as I wiped away my tears while smiling warmly at A'Miracle before returning Justin's gaze. Justin looked at me with those thoughtful, deep green eyes and told me with his eyes that he would never communicate with his words. Deep in his eyes I saw the same pain I kept just beyond the surface along with great concern. Justin wouldn't admit it but deep down he knew I was planning something, and he knew I wouldn't stop until Abaddon was dead. He just didn't want to ruin that happy, safe little world we had created for ourselves, and neither did I. That is why I fought the feelings inside of me and worked to calm that inner rage. The love I saw in my daughter's eyes as she stood there smiling at me gave me what I needed, quickly filling me with the warmth of her love.

Suddenly I regained my composure and realized that the old, tattered dance outfit I had on the night we escaped from hell eight years earlier was still hanging in plain sight on the wall. Just as the realization became clearer in my mind Justin turned and looked directly at it. It was like he read my mind, or better yet like always he heard my thoughts. My heart raced a mile a minute as I watched his body stiffen. The muscles in his neck bulged and veins popped out of his forehead as he clenched his teeth together. I knew Justin was remembering all of the times he had to do that same posture to defend me from Abaddon. In that second Justin was back there just as I had been, but I had to get him out. I had to break the spell and bring back that cool, rational Justin that got me through so many difficult nights. I couldn't have both of us falling apart at the seams. Who would look out for A'Miracle if both of us were insane? I couldn't let my baby become a lost child and possibly end up prey on the streets like I did. No, I could never let that happen, so I jumped into action, attempting to divert Justin's attention and return his inner peace.

"Hey mommy's little miracle. How was your playdate with Tianna?" I asked my daughter as I walked over to her and swept her long, thin body up in my arms, kissing her on the cheeks.

I kept my eyes on Justin as I tickled A'Miracle and she giggled while trying to squirm away.

"I had fun mommy. We played cheerleader. I had fun so stop tickling me." A'Miracle giggled as I continued to tickle her but keeping my eyes on Justin who was still standing there staring at the outfit on the wall.

I had seen that trance several times before. I knew Justin was in a dark place only my love could rescue him from, and I was right there to save him.

"What about daddy. Did daddy have fun?" I asked while giggling as I let A'Miracle go and quickly ran over to Justin and began tickling him.

As soon as my hands touched Justin's sides I felt his body relax. I tickled him in his sides and stomach as A' Miracle laughed, and a small smile appeared on his face. Despite that, Justin still continued to look at the outfit on the wall.

"Daddy, did you have fun; because if you didn't mommy has a fast, fun-filled game for you right now." I said to Justin as I wrapped one arm around his waist and used the other to turn his head towards me.

When I met Justin's eerie gaze his green eyes looked dull with flickers of anger dancing around in them. The muscles in his jaws relaxed a little as I pulled his face down to me and kissed him gently on the lips before whispering in his ear.

"I'm sorry baby. I had to keep it...I had to remember. I'll get rid of it now though. I don't need it anymore. All I need is you and A'Miracle...my family." I whispered sincerely to Justin in his ear before facing him again and he stared at me with glossy eyes.

Justin shook his head yes before I kissed him again with more passion and love. I had to let him know that I was still the Jess he needed me to be. I sighed with relief when I felt his arms encircle me tightly and felt his warm, sweet tongue on mine. A'Miracle broke our tender embrace within seconds as she laughed and moaned in disgust.

"Ewwwwww mommy and daddy please stop. That is so gross." A'Miracle whined causing Justin and I both to stop kissing and laugh.

A'Miracle stood there looking adorable in her pink shorts and white tank top with pink butterflies all over it as she scrunched up her nose and backed away. She was beautiful with her fair skin, long, thick black hair and big, deep dark eyes. I hated to admit it, but she looked just like Abaddon. I often wondered if Justin noticed that or ever thought about why A'Miracle had none of his features like his green eyes or blonde hair. If Justin did ever question it he never let me know. He was A'Miracle's knight in shining armor. In her eyes her daddy was the best and he could do no wrong. I could never break that beautiful bond my husband and our daughter shared, which is why I HAD to kill Abaddon. I had to get rid of him for good and make sure he never popped up in our lives again. I had to protect that precious angel from the treacherous, evil other side of her and keep my family together. I just couldn't let Justin know what I was doing.

Justin and I broke our embrace while laughing as A' Miracle continued to grimace at the thought of us kissing.

"Well since you hate to see your mommy and daddy give sugar, you give me some then." Justin said as he swept A'Miracle up in his arms and kissed her all over her face.

I felt tears well up in my eyes as I watched my husband pour more love on to his daughter than I ever thought possible. I was so happy in that moment, I only wished that happiness would last forever. However, I knew that just below my happiness was an insanely intense rage that I couldn't keep buried. I had to satisfy that thirst for revenge and ensure my daughter would be safe forever.

"Now run up stairs and get whatever you want to take to the park later. We are going to go out to eat then spend the rest of the afternoon in the park. Just A'Miracle, her mommy, and her daddy. What about that little miss Butterfly?" Justin asked A'Miracle as he put her down on the steps.

A'Miracle beamed with excitement as she rocked back and forth on her heels and giggled.

"Yes I'm getting ready daddy. Let's go to the water park. I want to wear the new Hello Kitty swimsuit mommy got me…...Then we'll have dessert in the park. Yess...this is going to be so much fun!! Love you Mommy. Love you daddy." A'Miracle squealed as she quickly turned to run up the stairs and to her room.

I stood there smiling for a minute, staring at the back of Justin's head as he watched A'Miracle disappear upstairs. Justin didn't move a muscle until A'Miracle was completely gone and we could hear her laughter and footsteps as she ran across the hardwood floor above. Just then Justin turned around slowly to face me with fire in his eyes and tears on his cheeks. I ran over to him quickly and buried my head in his chest as he held me tightly and kissed the top of the head.

"What is it Jess? Are you not happy with me? Am I not helping to erase the pain and the memories of the past?" Justin asked me sincerely as I looked up at him and wiped away his tears.

I hated to see him like that, suffering because I was still holding on to so much hurt and pain. I wished I could be like him and secretly deal with the pain and be able to let it go and live normally. However, I just couldn't. I couldn't let it go and completely move on. Knowing Abaddon was alive made me feel like I could be a victim again at any time and I couldn't live with that. I just couldn't say that to Justin, not yet anyway.

"Of course you make me happy baby. Justin, I love you and our daughter more than anything in this world. I just still hold on to some old feelings. It's hard sometimes to let go of the hate, but I'm getting better baby. Your love and A'Miracle's love are the only things that get me through. All I need is my family. That's it." I lied to my husband with tears burning behind my eyes.

I hated to lie to my husband, but I knew in that moment that was what he needed to hear. That was also what I needed to hear myself say in order to stifle my rage and live happy in the moment with my family. My time for revenge would soon come. Indeed, it would, but I had to be patient and give all of the love I had to my daughter and husband in the meantime. They deserved that much just in case I never came home again.

Justin hugged me tighter to him and kissed me on my head as I sighed. "Well let's just be happy Jess. Let's just stay in this little world we created for ourselves and leave all of the heartache in the past. You need to relax more. Next week you're taking a mini vacation. Why don't you call up Maria and get your sorority sister Kelen and go to Atlantic City or Vegas for a week. I will take care of A'Miracle. You need some time to unwind and enjoy yourself. You deserve the world baby - you take care of everyone else. Let me pamper you for a change. I love you baby and I'll always be here, never forget that." Justin said as he wiped away the single happy tear that had escaped his eye.

I just felt so blessed to have someone like Justin in my life and even though we met under terrible circumstances, I knew that he was the man made just for me. Suddenly, I flashed back to that wonderful September day that Justin and I were married. I remembered walking down the aisle to my dream guy standing there looking so handsome in his white tux with champagne colored bow tie as our beautiful one-year old daughter held his hand. That was the happiest day of my life and after seven years of blissful marriage, I loved him more at that moment than I ever had. He still made my heart flutter when he said my name. His touch still ignited a fire deep inside of me only his love could quench. Just then I felt an overwhelming need to feel Justin's arms around me. I needed to feel him inside of me. I stared at my husband with lust in my eyes before licking the corners of my mouth and biting my bottom lip. Justin returned the lust filled look, staring into my soul as he gripped my ass and pulled me into a deep kiss. Before I knew it, Justin had picked me up as I wrapped my legs around his waist. The passion between us was so strong we both moaned in pleasure as we kissed and vowed to love one another forever.

Justin carried me over to our second laundry room in the far corner behind the steps and sat me on top of the dryer before stepping back. I followed his sculptured body with my eyes as he took off his pants and boxers leaving them at his feet. He stood before me with his long, thick, vanilla manhood throbbing as my body yearned for his touch. I reached my arms out for him while biting my bottom lip as he came to me, kissing me on my face, down my neck, resting on my left breast. I bit down on my finger trying to muffle my moans as Justin kissed down my stomach while pulling my Nike running shorts and panties off. Before I could protest Justin buried his face deep inside of me, sending jolts of electricity and muscle spasms all through my body with every flick of his tongue. I felt as if my body was on fire as Justin kissed and tasted me while gazing up into my eyes.

"I love you forever Jess...always have." Justin said as I grabbed him by the face, pulling him up to me.

Justin entered me gently as I scooted to the edge of the dryer, wrapping my legs around his waist. Justin and I made love on the dryer that day and I felt a passion purer, and more fulfilling than I ever knew possible. When it was over we both lay there on the basement floor just as we had eight years earlier in hell, and Justin held me in his arms while he caressed my hair. I felt that same sense of safety and peace I felt back then as Justin promised me once again everything would be alright. I allowed my husband to fool my brain in that moment and accepted that everything would be alright. However, in my heart that nagging feeling began to throb and fill me with anxious butterflies like it did many times before. I had to use all of my might to swallow down those screams inside and face the world with that brave face I was famous for.

Justin and I dressed and then went upstairs to shower before the water park. As I stood in the shower and the hot water beat down on me I tried to clear my mind of the menacing thoughts that consumed me. The entire time I dressed and prepared to leave with my family I kept telling myself that my time would come to get revenge. I knew that I just had to be patient.

"Just hold on Jess...it'll be your time soon." I told myself as I walked out of the door with my husband and daughter later, trying so hard to be patient.

I just had to stay calm and silence the rage a little longer and then I could get my revenge. Justin had given me the excuse I needed to begin my plan. That getaway with the girls he talked about would in fact be the escape I needed to purge. The time I needed to rid myself of the pain and hurt I carried inside. I would release all of that venom on to Abaddon and his boys, and then I would come back home renewed, satisfied, and confident that my family was safe. All that was left for me to do was wait. I could do that.

****

Lunch with A'Miracle and Justin was great. I sat in a daze several times just staring at my daughter's face and seeing the love her and her father shared. We giggled and played while enjoying each other's company until everyone's stomach was stuffed with pizza, pasta, and cheesy breadsticks. After eating, Justin and I sat and watched A'Miracle play the games in the restaurant's game room; bouncing around in a cloud of happiness, oblivious to the pain and hurt out in the world. Justin and I had done a great job at only showing her the best...the good, which was why I was so afraid of her ever having to visit my type of past. I just wanted to grab her in my arms and hold her forever as she ran over to me with that big, beautiful smile.

"Mommy my bows came out when I went into the tunnels." A'Miracle said with the sad face as she held her crumbled butterfly bows in her hand.

I quickly swooped in to the rescue as I usually did, bending the soft metal back into shape before placing all four bows back into her hair. A'Miracle shook and bounced in joy after looking in the mirror on the restaurant wall and seeing the perfect butterflies sticking in her hair before quickly running away. She always got excited like that when butterflies were involved. She loved butterflies from the moment she was old enough to say the word. Like me with dance she said looking at butterflies made her feel free. That's probably why she inherited my natural talent for dance, in all butterfly attire of course. At almost eight years old A'Miracle was more disciplined, focused, and gifted than I was at 20 and back then I had a full scholarship to Juilliard, which I turned down to study criminal psychology. That was because after living in hell, I just couldn't look at dancing the same anymore. Abaddon had spoiled that for me with his sick, perverse sex games. Every time I tried to dance in front of someone knowingly I felt like their eyes were his, burning through my clothes, my skin, and straight to my soul. The psychological scars he left on me were too deep to move on and dance without remembering. That is why I began to research psychology. At first I wanted to find out what was wrong with me and fix myself, but then I realized nothing was wrong with me. It was Abaddon who was rotten to the core and needed to be fixed or erased. That is what I told myself and after that realization criminal psychology just fell into my lap. Once I finished school and began working in the field the first year I wondered why I ever wanted to dance instead. However, after seeing A'Miracle's natural talent in dance, I began to miss it more. It was later that it dawned on me that I could live through her. By watching her I was sometimes able to feel that same release, that sense of freedom and connectedness I used to feel when I would dance. That was a wonderful feeling I probably would never forget.

After dinner we went to the amusement park and spent hours riding rides and eating funnel cakes, candy apples, and cotton candy until we all felt nauseous. I had to make my little hyper butterfly take a breather after that because I was about to die. I conned her into playing instead of riding rides so that I could rest. To my surprise she fell for it and let us lead her to the fenced in play area. Justin and I sat on a bench in front of the playground inside of the fairground and watched A'Miracle play with the other kids. It was refreshing sitting there in my husband's arms while watching our daughter, run and play like a child without a care in the world. She didn't know the dangers that lurked around each corner nor the changes that would come. That was just something that she could not foresee and in reality, none of us did.

As we sat there, I kissed my husband gently on the neck and turned back to my daughter who was going up the slide. I watched her naturally elegant self-climb those steps on her toes and the dancer and mom in me felt proud. In the mist of my admiration I watched a boy who appeared to be about 10 suddenly appear and grab A'Miracle by her leg, pulling her back down the slide. She was only up two steps, so she didn't fall far, but in the process her hair did get caught on a piece of metal in the handle. That snag under her weight caused her head to jerk back and she instantly screamed out in pain. After seeing that my natural mommy instinct was to jump up and run to my daughter. If I had of, I probably would have punched the little fat, rosy cheeked, Brian Griffin looking boy who pulled her down right in his eye. However, Justin didn't let me. As soon as I stood up to sprint over, Justin grabbed me by the back of my wrap skirt and pulled me back down on to the bench beside him.

"No love, let her handle it herself. We can't always be there for her. She has to learn to protect herself." Justin said giving me a reassuring look as I looked at him back like he had lost his mind.

On the inside I knew Justin was right, although I just wanted to wiggle out of his grip and run to save my baby. I couldn't do that though. I knew it was important for her to be able to handle herself. I just hoped she would never have to do the things I had to do when trying to survive against the devil. That's why, reluctantly, I sat back down beside Justin and watched A'Miracle as she stood at the bottom of the slide with her arms folded and pouted. I fought the urge to jump up again as Justin held me in his arms, still reassuring me.

"If she looks at us we turn our head." Justin said as A'Miracle instantly turned our way.

It took everything in me to turn away from her with Justin, but I did despite the fact I didn't want to. I quickly turned back around just as the little chubby boy ran back around the slide to climb back up. A'Miracle was still standing there pouting as he threw a finger sign at her on his way up. Suddenly I saw A'Miracle take on a familiar, sinister posture that made my flesh crawl. Her shoulders looked so broad and solid she could have been a mini body builder. I watched as her chest raised up and fell in great heaves as she clenched her fists and gritted her teeth, breathing hard and grunting at the same time. Her eyes were so dark, evil, and intense in that moment, I knew for sure my Butterfly, my angel was indeed the child of the devil, Abaddon. I glanced over at Justin for a second as he stared straight ahead with a stunned and quizzical look on his face. When I looked back at A'Miracle I was totally taken aback as I watched her charge forward, grabbing the boy by both legs and pulling him face down, all the way to the bottom of the slide steps. I looked on frozen in horror as the boy's face and chin hit each step on the way down and blood squirted out of his nose and mouth. The boy grabbed his mouth and then he noticed the blood dripping from his face before he yelled out in pain. I watched my angel snicker at the boy as she stood back with her arms crossed with a satisfied expression on her face. That look, and her demeanor made me feel cold and scared. That's why I jumped up and kept my eyes on A'Miracle as I walked towards her in a daze while Justin and other parents ran past me. I watched as my daughter leaned down and whispered something in the boy's ear as she held him firmly in the back of his curly blonde hair. By the time Justin and the other parents made it to them A'Miracle was rubbing the boy's hair and acting as if she was trying to comfort him. I looked on stunned as I continued to walk towards my daughter who had backed up but was still staring at the boy angrily as he was being comforted by his parents. A'Miracle had a tight, cold expression on her face as she intimidated the boy who was twice her size simply using the evil she had inside. I felt chills run up and down my spine and goose bumps pop up all over my body as my daughter continued to stare the bloody, crying boy down.

I could do nothing as I watched Justin go over to A'Miracle after checking on the boy and begin to ask her what happened and why she had done what she did. By that time, I was standing right in front of them as I watched my daughter quickly replace that cold, hateful look she inherited from Abaddon with the happy, innocent face we knew and loved. I was amazed at how manipulative and sneaky she could be as I stood by quietly and watched her work her magic on her daddy to get herself out of a sticky situation.

"Daddy I don't know what happened. I was playing, and he pushed me down, but I let that go. After that I was just standing there, and he ran by throwing a finger sign at me. Next thing I know he was going up the steps and suddenly came tumbling back down. He was like Jack and Jill when they fell down that hill daddy. Only he didn't have a Jill." A'Miracle said in an innocent yet sarcastic manner that made my heart flutter.

I felt myself grow tense as I listened to my daughter lie to us like it was nothing. However, even though that was bad, that wasn't what bothered me the most. What really got to me was the fact that she was so cool and calculated under pressure. I hated to admit it or even think it, but she had inherited so much darkness from Abaddon it was hard for me not to see it. She was this innocent soul with an evil streak that she couldn't even explain. That's why I had to stop that hate from consuming her, so I stepped forward to ask her myself. I felt like she couldn't look me in the eye and lie to me, so in an effort to give a chance to be truthful, I asked her again. I asked her twice using different wording and after getting the same, I don't know, response I was about to lose my patience with my baby. Just then the boy's mother walked over and informed me that her son admitted that he fell and A'Miracle was trying to help him. She said that her son was accident prone, so seeing him take a fall wasn't unusual. I didn't know what to say at that point because I knew what I had seen and in my heart, I knew what my child had done. I knew my angel has struck back; harder and with more malice, and then threatened the boy to keep quiet. That's why I looked at Justin and then my daughter before turning back to the woman. She informed me that her son's injuries were minor before she naïvely thanked A'Miracle for helping.

"Thank you so much pretty young lady for helping my son." the woman said smiling as she shook A'Miracle's hand.

I watched my daughter con her too as she gave her the sweetest, most innocent smile she could find

"Oh no ma'am, you don't have to thank me. I was just doing what I was supposed to. I hope your son gets better. Can I go over to tell him I hopes he feels better before you take him to the hospital?" A'Miracle asked the woman with a big do-eyed look.

My daughter was being a little psychopath right before my eyes and I couldn't believe it.

"No, A'Miracle he has to go get treatment. His mother will tell him what you said." I told my daughter, grabbing her by the shoulders as I glanced from her to Justin.

Justin just stood there looking as confused as I felt inside. He knew what he saw, but I could tell he was questioning that after hearing A'Miracle's side of the story. Hell, she was so convincing I was starting to question what I saw too, although my mind told me I was right. Luckily, the lady agreed they had to get going before rushing away. After that our day of fun was over, so I quickly gathered my things before returning to my husband and daughter, and we exited the park. On our way to the car we walked past the boy's parents van just as they rode by. The boy sat in the rear holding a towel to his mouth and chin as he stared out of the window. Justin walked ahead to unlock the car doors as I held A'Miracle's hand, and we strolled slowly and quietly. Just as the boy's car made it pass us I looked up to see A'Miracle hold her finger to her lips to silence the boy while she glared him down. I watched astonished as the boy scooted down in his seat and hid his face from A'Miracle's evil glare. I felt her body stiffen as she continued to glare at him then soften before she smirked then looked up at me. In that moment she saw me staring at her and she knew I saw what she did. She tried to hide her eyes from me as we continued to walk, but I saw what I knew I saw when she pulled the boy down the slide. I saw a rage that was uncontrollable and the desire to inflict pain. In that moment I knew that Abaddon had given my daughter some of the worst and most devious parts of him. Parts she could keep hidden until she needed them and could use them to her advantage. I hated Abaddon for that, and I couldn't wait to make him pay once and for all.

The car ride home after A'Miracle's incident was quiet and eerie. I couldn't help but to think about the look in her eyes and how manipulative and evil she could be. I was so consumed with my thoughts as I listened to her sing along to the radio from the backseat I didn't even hear Justin calling my name.

"JESSICA... What's wrong?" Justin yelled startling me out of my deep, dark thoughts.

I was happy he had interrupted the horrible scenes that were playing out in my mind, in which A'Miracle was just like Abaddon, a monster. I wanted to shake those thoughts and the visions of her face looking distorted and evil, but they kept flashing before my eyes. I managed to shake them though and that eerie feeling that loomed over me as I looked over at Justin.

"Yes baby, I'm sorry. My mind was totally somewhere else right now. What is it though love?" I asked Justin in the fakest, happiest voice I could produce as he stared at me unconvinced that I was okay.

I could feel his eyes burning the side of my face as I turned away, sat up in my seat and peered at A'Miracle through the rearview mirror. My baby smiled at me with the sweetest, most loving smile I had ever seen, melting my heart and causing me to return the love. I didn't want to be mad at, scared of, or stand-offish with my daughter, but it was clear to me that she had a powerful evil lurking inside of her that I had to keep buried. I had to do what I had to do to keep her safe and divert her away from that evil she had inherited. I knew I just had to figure out how to do that without alerting Justin as I looked back over at him after smiling at A'Miracle and I saw the same concern on his face that I had in his eyes. I knew that he had seen the same things I saw when he looked at the daughter we adored. I also knew that Justin was finally ready to talk about why the evil we both saw in her was there. I dreaded that inevitable talk in which I would have to admit to the love of my life that our daughter was not his, but instead that man who had taken our innocence. I had gone over that speech a thousand times in my head from a million different angles, and each time I saw myself falling apart. However, when Justin smiled at me warmly and reached over to grab my hand, I knew that everything would be fine. Just like he had promised me almost a decade before, I knew that Justin would always stand by my side no matter what.

"Don't worry Jess…I know! She has more of us in her though, so everything will work out. Just believe it and keep giving her all the love you can. We are going to do this together. Okay?" Justin asked me as a single tear fell from my eye.

I sucked up those screams inside and quickly wiped away my tear with the back of my hand before leaning over to kiss Justin behind his ear. I felt at peace again, at least for that moment. However, that peace didn't last long because once we got home and I put A'Miracle to bed my mind wandered back to her incident in the park and the Amber Alert for the missing girl. For some reason those two things seemed related to me, probably because of Abaddon. Whatever the reason was I couldn't take my mind off of it as I sat in my living room in the middle of my huge black sectional and played the news report again on my DVR. This time while watching the news report I paid close attention to the names of the two girls who reported Mikayla missing. I quickly jumped up after memorizing their names and ran into my office to grab my laptop. I tiptoed back into the living room trying not to wake Justin or A'Miracle as I opened my laptop and logged in to Facebook. As I sat down I quickly entered the first girl's name and went directly to her page. I went down her wall looking at all of the pictures of her and her friends. As I scrolled down the page a picture of Mikayla caught my eye and I almost died. It was like I was looking at myself in the mirror almost. Mikayla shared a distinct resemblance to me at her age and aside from that she was a dancer too. In the picture she had on a black leotard with black tights and white ballet shoes, looking graceful as she plied. Chills went up and down my spine as I studied the picture of the beautiful teen with her long black hair flowing in the wind as my heart raced. I felt connected to Mikayla at that moment, and I knew that no matter what happened I had to save her like I was saved. Before I knew it I had sent the girl a message asking to speak to her about Mikayla. I did the same thing to the other girl as my mind moved a mile a minute and I felt those familiar butterflies fluttering in my stomach up to my heart. I could sense something was about to happen. It was like I could feel my moment for revenge getting nearer and that knowledge made me anxious and a bit afraid. I just hoped I would be able to do what needed to be done when the time came.

After waiting around for the girls to respond for few minutes, I closed my laptop and tip-toed upstairs to bed. I made a quick stop at A'Mircale's room, opening her door and peeking in. She looked so innocent and peaceful asleep in her huge princess canopy bed with fluffy, pink butterfly covers. I just wanted to freeze her in that moment forever and prevent any hurt or harm from coming her way. I knew that was an unrealistic dream, but I had hope that I would at least be able to keep her away from Abaddon. I had to.

I closed A'Miracles door and then tip-toed to my own, opening it quietly, and slipping into the room. I glanced at Justin laying on his side facing the wall before slipping into bed beside him. I laid there with my eyes open for a few seconds, staring up at the ceiling thinking about what my next week would be like when Justin suddenly began to talk.

"Jess, I know A'Miracle is not my biological daughter." Justin said, stopping my heart and causing tears to well up in my eyes.

I felt my entire body tense up as the realization of what Justin said resonated in my mind. As tears began falling from my eyes, Justin turned facing me still laying on his side and propping his head up with his hand. He stared into my eyes through the darkness like he had done many nights before when we were trapped in hell. He reached out and wiped away my tears before pulling me into his arms as I buried my face in his chest. He kissed the top of my head and squeezed me tight as I felt his body shudder around me.

"It's okay Jess. I've always known she was Abaddon's, I'm not blind Jessica." Justin said through his tears as I held my head up to look into his sad, hurt eyes.

I just wanted to take away all of the pain he felt at that moment as I wiped away the tears that had begun falling heavily from his eyes.

"Justin please, I'm so sorry baby." I began as Justin put his finger to my lips to cut me off.

"Don't you dare apologize Jess. You have nothing to apologize for. He did what he did to you against your will. There was nothing you could have done to stop it, but I should have. I should have got you out of there sooner and for that I am sorry baby. However, I don't ever want to hear you apologize from bringing one of the most important women in my life into this world. You gave me the gift of fatherhood Jess and I am forever grateful. A'Miracle will never know about this, and we will live our lives happily ever after. Okay?" Justin asked me as he smiled and kissed my eyes.

I wanted to just forget the butterflies in my stomach and the nagging feeling in my heart, but I couldn't. I couldn't let that moment just move forward without addressing the issues that concerned me most, and that was A'Miracle.

"Yes baby, I want to just move on too, but what about what we saw today? She has more of him in her than I ever noticed. How can we ensure she doesn't end up being a predator just like him?" I asked Justin through my tears as they continued to fall, and he looked me intensely in the eyes.

I didn't want to believe that my child, the baby I had, could be as evil as the sadistic monster who took pleasure in abusing and killing children. However, after seeing her do what she had done that day, I knew that it was possible. I knew that if in the right circumstance my daughter could be just as cold and callus as her biological father, and that is was what sent jolts of fear to my core.

"I know what you saw Jess because I saw it too. I don't know what we have to do to suppress that side of her other than love her, but what I do know is that we will do it together. A'Miracle is OUR child and children are often a product of their environment. As long as we continue to provide a loving, happy, supportive, positive home life she will be just fine. Trust me baby. Now close your weary eyes and rest your beautiful mind. Daddy got you." Justin said as he wrapped me in his arms again and kissed me on the forehead.

The nagging feeling in my heart slowly disappeared as I laid in Justin's arms listening to his heartbeat and breathing in tune with him. I wanted to believe everything he said was true, but the butterflies fluttering in my stomach told me that there was way more mayhem to come. I ignored that feeling though and closed my eyes tight in an attempt to go to sleep. I laid there for an hour or so before sleep finally found me, whisking me into a series of terrible dreams.

I woke up the next morning feeling weighed down with those same butterflies still in my stomach. My mind was stuck on A'Miracle's incident and Mikayla being missing. After fixing breakfast for my family and getting dressed for church I slipped into my office to check my Facebook for a message from the girl. As soon as I logged in and the message icon popped up on the screen my heart began to race, and I felt light-headed. I had to sit down as I clicked the message from the first girl and read it to myself. She had given me her cell number and told me she could meet with me that afternoon. I quickly took out my phone and saved her number before texting to let her know who I was. After confirming a 3 pm lunch date with her at the I-Hop close by her home, I turned off my phone and prepared to leave for church with my family.

When we got to church I put all of my anxiety, anger, and fear on the back burner as I put on a brave face for the world like I always did. No one, but Justin knew the pain and turmoil I still held inside and not even he knew the plan I had cooking. I sat through the service lost in my own thoughts, anticipating my meeting with the girl.

Towards the end of the service I finally snapped back into reality just as my pastor talked about releasing negative energy and filling up on positive. He said there was no way man could be happy carrying around pain, hurt, anger, and fear everywhere they went. He said you have to leave that baggage behind and walk away in order to find that happiness God promised. A single tear fell from my eye as I listened because it seemed he was talking directly to me. I knew that I needed to let my feelings go, however; I thought that the only way I would be able to do that was by getting rid of Abaddon and whoever else was associated with him. That was the only way I felt I could ever find happiness. I wish I would have thought on it a little more and asked the Most High for guidance, but I didn't.

I dismissed that voice in my head telling me to rethink things as I looked out of the window on our drive home. I pretended everything was alright as I went home and prepared football snacks for my fanatic husband and daughter. I knew that they both would be too preoccupied with games all day to worry about me so that was the perfect opportunity for me to slip away. After delivering their snacks and stealing kisses I ran upstairs to change quickly. I dressed in black cotton capris, a yellow tank top, and matching tennis shoes before saying goodbye to my family again and leaving the house.

I drove to the I-Hop in the subdivision next to mine with nothing but thoughts of revenge running through my mind. I imagined myself torturing Abaddon the same way that he did us. There was nothing else in the world I wanted more than to show Abaddon that pain went two ways, and he was not above feeling it. I got to the I-Hop which was 10 minutes away from my home, in about six minutes flat, anxious to get my first piece of the puzzle. When I walked into the restaurant Mikayla's best friends Ariana and Krystal were the first two people I saw. I walked over and gave both girls a hug after introducing myself, then we all sat down.

"First I would just like to thank both of you brave young ladies for agreeing to speak with me. I have had a personal interest in your friend's disappearance since the story broke and I would really like to help find her…or at least try. So I am going to ask you both now, with no judgment or accusations, is there anything you all haven't told yet?" I asked both girls as I watched tears well up in their eyes and they shook their heads no.

I knew right then that they held the key to me finding Mikayla and eventually finding Abaddon, I just had to get the information out of them. I knew how it felt to be afraid to talk, but I had to make them understand that something way more important than being labeled as a rat was at stake. I had to make them see that Mikayla's life depended on them and that I was probably the only person who could save her. To do that I knew I had to make them understand why Mikayla's case was so important to me. I knew that I had to tell them my story.

"Listen babies, I know how it is. No one wants to be a rat and you all have loyalty to your friend to keep her secrets. However, you all have to understand Mikayla's life could depend on this. When I was about y'all age I thought I had it all figured out too. I wanted to be on my own, make my own decisions, and just be grown. So my best friend and I ran away to Las Vegas and for weeks we lived our dream. I even met my now husband on the strip one night. Now after all the glamour we ended up broke and on the streets until two fine guys saved us. They took us in and took care of us, baiting us in to their plan. Before long everything changed, and we ended up chained by our wrists in a tracker trailer truck with 20-30 other kids headed to New York for sex trafficking. We were beaten, raped, tortured, sold, and some killed. I lost my best friend while in that hell and so did my husband. We made a choice to change our lives and ended up causing ourselves nothing but pain. We were held by a man who is more evil than the devil himself, and I think that same man has your friend. Now I ask you again, are you going to help me save her?" I said to the girls as tears fell from my cheeks.

I was so wrapped up in my story I didn't even realize I was crying until I felt the warm tears drip down my shirt. I watched as tears fell from both of the girls' eyes as they held hands and the first girl I contacted, Ariana, pulled a red folder out of her purse.

"I'm so sorry for everything that happened to you and you losing your friend, but I don't want that to happen to my friend. There are some things we haven't told anyone, and I just hope it's not too late. Here is every message she sent to the mystery boyfriend on her secret Facebook account." Ariana said as she passed me the folder and I quickly opened it, glancing over the pages of messages.

"She had been talking to him a long time and he always tried to get to her so urgently. I think that's why I never liked him because he was too eager and told the most elaborate stories about him being a European model who moved to America to work for some big Russian crime boss. He was just a fucking creep to me and now I know why. Please find our friend Ms. Jessica. Please!" Krystal begged me as I sat the folder on the table and then I reached out to grab both of their hands.

"I promise you both I will do all I can to find her, just don't give up hope. And please be safe and protect each other because there are predators out here." I said to the girls before standing, hugging them both as I grabbed the folder and left.

When I made it to my car I couldn't wait to open the folder again and start reading. I read through the pages of messages quickly and thoroughly, being sure not to miss a thing. There was something so familiar about the way this guy who's name was supposed to be Jabari, was talking to Mikayla. I quickly recognized the manipulation and felt a familiar sickness in the pit of my stomach. When I read him call her sweet lady several times I knew that my suspicions were true and the guy who took Mikayla was in fact Tony. The same evil bastard who had manipulated me into trusting him by acting like he loved me only to hand me over to the devil had done the same thing to Mikayla. I was guessing that simply getting runaways and snatching kids out of their beds had become too boring for them. Now they were using mind tricks and coercion to get the kids to come to them. That shit made me so mad I had to punch my steering wheel before continuing to read. On the next to the last page I got the tab bit of information I needed to find the first sick fuck and get closer to saving Mikayla. There was a message on that page from the fucker that said how much he wanted to take care of her and show her all Vegas had to offer. He was still in Vegas, probably still working with Mark, luring in young girls to deliver them to the devil. The thought of returning to that place made me afraid, but anxious at the same time. I knew I would have to face that fear one day, and the time had come. I wasn't going to be the victim this time though. I was going to transform all of that fear and anxiety I felt inside into hate, malice, and a deep desire to inflict pain. I was about to go from prey to predator, and I was ready.

"Vegas huh? Well, I'm on my way back there too then bitch! See you when I get there Tony. Your hell is about to begin!" I said to myself as I closed the folder, throwing it into the passenger seat before I headed home to start my trip.

I drove home still wrapped in my thoughts. All I could think of was what might have been happening to Mikayla in Tony's evil, manipulative hands. I could remember like yesterday how loving and kind he was to me when we first met, buying Quintika and me clothes and food and getting us off the street. We thought that he and Mark were our saviors only to find out that it was all a game. They baited us in and made us vulnerable just like they wanted, and then when our guards were all the way down they changed. I can still remember the evil in his eyes that night after he drugged me, and I can still feel the searing pain in my cheek after he slapped me and called me a slutty little rich girl. That was the worse night of my life and the beginning of my hell, which is something I would never forget. I hated Tony and Mark for what they had done, and I wanted nothing more than to make them feel the pain I felt.

"Your time is coming fucker…believe me." I said out loud to myself as glanced at the folder one last time before putting it into the glove compartment.

By the time I got home I had buried all of those old memories and feelings deep inside and put on a brave face. I spent the rest of the evening on the couch with my daughter and husband, just enjoying their presence. After kissing A'Miracle and putting her to bed, I went to take a shower and prepare for my trip. As the hot water from the shower rained down on me, filling me with warmth I felt an overwhelming sense of sorrow envelope me. All that I could think about was those days I had to shower in that filthy bathroom with rusty water and perverted, piercing eyes wandering all over my body. For a second I was that little girl again, cowering in the corner wishing the madness would end. I must have gotten too engulfed in my memories and pain because the next thing I knew I felt the shower door open, and Justin was standing there in his blue cotton boxers asking me what was wrong.

"Jess baby, what's wrong?" Justin asked as I turned around to him fully revealing my tears.

Looking into his loving, concerned eyes I couldn't hide my pain, so I just released it all as I cried out and my body shook. Justin quickly stepped into the shower in his boxers and took me in his arms, kissing away my tears and promising to protect me like he had always did. I wiped away my sorrow as he kissed and held me while telling me how much he loved me.

"Please Jess, stop it. Don't let your memories control you anymore. We have moved past all of that, Abaddon doesn't win. You are successful, intelligent, and a great wife and mother. You win Jess. WE win, not him. I love you Mrs. Jessica Michaels. I love you more than life itself. Hell, you and A'Miracle are my life. We need you to be okay. We need you to let the pain go. He only wins if we let him effect the way we live Jess. Go on your trip tomorrow, have fun with your friends, and come back happy and free of your demons. Come back to me as the Jessica I married. I need you baby." Justin said to me as tears fell from his eyes and the shower water washed them away.

At that moment I looked up into my husband's beautiful green eyes and found the strength that I needed. His love helped to mask my pain and allow myself a second of peace. I kissed my husband with so much love and passion that it took him by surprise as I pushed him into the stone shower wall. I felt a fire ignite between my legs as I thought about how much my husband loved me. I knew that after all of the tragedy we had gone through it was a miracle we had found each other and fell in love.

I kissed down Justin's chest to his abs before grabbing the waist band of his soaking wet boxers, quickly pulling them down to his ankles. I watched as the sorrow in his eyes changed to pure excitement while I took all of his throbbing manhood into my mouth. I deep throated my husband's 10-inch vanilla pleasure stick and moaned while looking up into his eyes. Justin was in heaven as he grabbed the back of my head and moved me up and down his shaft. I made small, fast circles around the head of his penis before blowing on it and then inserting it all into my mouth again. After doing that several more times Justin quickly pulled me up to him, kissing me hard, and passionately as he lifted me up and wedged me between his body and the stone shower wall. Justin kissed me passionately as he entered me, holding me up by my thighs. I felt as if my body was on fire as we smashed our bodies together and my passion grew. Justin and I made love in our shower that night as nothing but our love consumed my mind. When it was all over we gently, and lovingly washed one another before heading to bed.

I fell asleep naked that night in my husband's arms, wishing that moment could last forever. However, I knew that nothing lasted forever. Soon my happiness, peace, and tranquility would be filled with malice, violence, and revenge. I was leaving my house as Jessica the recovering victim, prey, but I would return a predator, the executioner.

The next morning I woke up feeling slightly off, but anxious to get my trip going. Visions of Tony's conniving face flashed before my eyes, igniting an anger inside of me that was hard to contain. I had to remind myself several times that my opportunity to deal with Tony was coming as I prepared and ate breakfast with my family. I hid the malice burning in my eyes from Justin as I pretended to laugh at his jokes and smiled at our beautiful daughter. Although physically my body was right there before them, my mind was miles away preparing a trap for the bastard who handed me to the devil.

I had went over my plan in my mind a dozen times and I was anxious to see it through. I just had to get past Justin without raising his suspicion. I almost made it too, however after dropping A'Miracle off at school Justin caught me in one of my quiet, staring moods. Usually whenever Justin caught me quiet for any period of time he knew it meant that something had triggered me, and I was reliving my pain. The only difference that time was that something had turned that pain off inside of me and replaced it with pure malevolence. No longer would I be that scared little girl hiding behind Justin or that fragile, vulnerable woman still haunted by the past. I was actually planning my revenge and to get it I would transform into a more terrifying monster than Abaddon, if I could get past Justin.

"Jess, what's going on with you? I know what that look means, and you've been quiet since we dropped A'Miracle off. Why are you reliving it again Jess?" Justin asked startling me out of my daydream of mutilating Tony.

I quickly shook off my evil thoughts as I managed a fake smile after turning to look at my husband. Justin's eyes were sincere and concerned as he tried to look through me and read my mind as he always did. I broke his gaze, quickly looking away and not allowing him to read me as he had grown accustomed to doing of the years. I wanted to completely protect him and A'Miracle from what I was about to do so I couldn't let him figure out what I had planned. I had to lie to my husband, which was something I said I would never do again.

"Nothing's wrong with me love. I was just sitting here thinking about how far we've come. I'm not reliving the past baby, I'm very much in the present and looking forward to our future, that's all." I said before scooting closer to Justin and kissing him on his neck, right behind his ear.

I felt his body relax some after the kiss, however, when I sat back up right in my seat I could still see some concern in his eyes. It was like Justin knew I was up to something, but he never said anything. We rode home, making small talk with one another as I enjoyed a little time with my one true love.

Once back at home I watched Justin take my bags to the car as I looked back one last time at my home. Suddenly an eerie feeling came over me and I couldn't help but to feel as if that would be my last time seeing the place I called home. Something, somewhere was telling me to leave the past where it was, but I just couldn't do that. Justin broke my thoughts as he walked back on to the porch and grabbed me in his arms, carrying me down to my car as he laughed and kissed me all over my face. His love and playfulness made me forget that eerie feeling that told me to stay home as I kissed him back and allowed him to place me in the car. After a couple of long passionate kisses and I love you's, I looked back at my husband as I pulled out of our driveway headed to I-15 towards Vegas.

I drove non-stop from L.A. to Baker, California in 2 hours, listening to the audio recordings I did when I created profiles on Abaddon, Tony, and Mark. The entire ride went by in a blur as I thought about the best way to torture Tony and find out where Mikayla was. I was consumed with those thoughts as my stomach started to growl and I glanced up to see a sign advertising the best gyros in the USA at the Mad Greek diner just off the next exit in the city of Baker. I quickly exited the interstate and pulled into the parking lot right in front of the big, blue and white castle-like structure with stone statues of Greek Gods all over it. I laughed as I got out of my car and walked inside to find a very clean and well-kept establishment. I ordered my cheeseburger, fries, and cherry coke and after getting my food I sat down close to the back door in a booth. I was enjoying the delicious food and quiet ambience just as a Caucasian teenage girl about 17-years-old burst through the back door. Her long blonde hair was all dirty and disheveled just like her clothing and the thick dark makeup around her eyes ran down her face in long, black streaks. Her eyes were blood shot red and she had a look of desperation that I had seen and felt before. I watched as she ran right past me over to the customers sitting at the counter, begging them for help or some change to use the phone. Everyone ignored her or either tried to get away from her like she had the plague or something. Just as I stood up to help the obviously traumatized girl a very large Caucasian man working as staff at the restaurant came from around the counter and roughly escorted the girl towards the door. I ran behind them and caught up just as the male employee pushed the girl out of the front doors and down to the ground before telling her to never bring her death metal, meth head ass back into his establishment. I stood there quietly right behind the fat asshole, raging inside until he turned around and stood face-to-face with me. Before he could say anything out of his fat, obnoxious mouth I grabbed his tiny penis in my hand using my death grip, digging my nails deep into his skin.

I don't know what came over me at that moment, but I was no longer the meek Jess I once was. All of that hate and pain I had carried inside for so long had manifested into something evil and totally destructive, and I was ready to unleash it on anyone who deserved it. The obnoxious, over-weight, poor excuse for a man in front of me at that moment was just a casualty, someone getting what they deserved. He let out a high-pitched scream so high I could barely hear it as I continued to squeeze his dick and balls in my hand while using my free hand to pull his head down so that I could whisper in his ear.

"Listen you rude fat fuck, obviously that girl needs help, so how about instead of being a worthless piece of shit you show some compassion. Or should I just rip this tiny, limp, half-eaten gummy worm off of your fucking body and ram it down your throat? The choice is yours, fat boy." I said to the fat, rude employee as I watched his face turn beet red.

I was sure he would pass out soon if I kept squeezing, but I really didn't give a fuck as I held his tiny dick and balls in my hand. It was time for payback, starting with him for being such a dick head. I smirked as the man began to whimper and the girl finally got up off of the ground. She ran over to us and began kicking and punching the fat dude as he continued to cry and whimper, and I squeezed a little harder. Within seconds I felt his large, flabby body go limp in my hands and I quickly stood back so that the big, flabby, mass of blubber he called a body wouldn't crush me on the way down. He hit the ground hard and fast making a loud thud as the girl and I stood there quiet and motionless. Suddenly I heard someone come out of the door and yell as I looked at the girl before sprinting away. I got to my car in two seconds without looking back while hitting my automatic door opener on my keys before getting there. I hopped into my car at the same time as the girl and instinctually started the car and sped out of the parking lot. I pushed my new Camaro to the dash as we whizzed down I-15, closer to La Vegas. For about 20 minutes we rode in silence as I watched my rearview mirror for the police or anyone following us. Soon my breathing became normal again and the butterflies in the pit of my stomach were gone so I turned to look at the girl who was sitting quietly in my passenger seat. I quickly looked the girl from top to bottom, noticing the bruises and cuts all over her body. I knew there was a story behind the way she looked, and I felt compelled to find out what had happened to land her at that restaurant.

"So what's your name?" I asked the girl as I glanced at her again from the corner of my eye.

I watched as tears and the thick black makeup ran down her cheeks and she turned to face me.

"Cassie." she said in a low, yet strong tone.

I could feel the hair on the back of my neck standup after hearing her name. Cassie was the name of one of the girl's killed in the truck with me when I was abducted. In that instant I could see visions of her face after Abaddon killed her, leaving her head print in blood on the truck wall. Rage rose up in me quick and hard as I thought about how she died in that truck beside her sister for no reason at all. I wished I could have done something to save Cassie and having another Cassie in need right there with me made me want to help again.

"Hi, Cassie. I'm Jess. So do you want to tell me what's going on so that I can figure out how to help?" I asked the girl as tears continued to fall from her eyes and she shook her head no.

I knew that there was something going on with her, something so bad it caused her to be all alone in the middle of nowhere, but I also knew I couldn't pressure her to talk. I had to let her tell me if I was going to be able to reach her and offer any help.

"It's okay, you don't have to tell me, until you are ready. It's another two hours between here and Vegas, so just know I'm all ears. We're not that different you know." I said to Cassie as she glanced at me out of curiosity. "Yeah I have scars and a story to tell too. Maybe someday we can tell each other our stories." I said to her as I reached down and pulled up my shirt revealing one of the many scars I acquired while trapped in hell.

I could see that Cassie wanted to talk by the way she kept glancing at me and then out of the window again, but she said nothing. Instead she leaned her head up against the window and drifted off to sleep. I focused on the road while getting lost in my thoughts, wondering where all of my new found strength and malice had come from. I got about 20 minutes outside of Las Vegas when the girl suddenly woke up and began telling me her story. I listened intently while paying close attention to the road as the girl told me about her parent's awful divorce and nasty custody battle. In the end she was left floating between her parents, spending half of each year with each parent. She told me how everything was alright at first but after two, six month stays with her father she noticed how he started drinking more and shortly after that the beatings began.

Cassie said that she told her mother about it and her mother threatened to go to the police, but her father took her and left before she could. She was eleven when that happened and everything in her life changed. Since then six years had passed and she said she had been a prisoner, a maid, nothing more than someone to hurt for her father and his new wife and kids. When she met me that day she said she had just gotten away from her father after he bashed her face into the dashboard for asking for something to eat on the way home from the family's dinner at which he wouldn't let her eat. She said she had planned to call her friend to get back to the house before them, get the little money she had stashed and disappear. After snooping on the internet she had found an address for a woman with the same name as her mother and she was going to go to Minnesota to be with her.

I could hear the desperation in her voice as she asked me to help her.

"Jess, can you help me. I see how ruthless you can be when provoked and I'll need someone like that if my dad shows up. Please, just go with me to get the money and then I'll disappear. However, if he shows up I know you will do what you have to do. Please Jess, do this for me and I will do anything you want." Cassie said through her tears as I contemplated what she said.

I quickly agreed to help Cassie after looking her in the eyes and seeing the urgency. It was like I was looking in the mirror as I glanced at familiar eyes with that same urgency I once had. I knew she needed my help and I figured I could use some help getting what I had come for. She would be good bait for a pedophile like Tony. It would be like I was killing two birds with one stone. Cassie gave me directions to her father's little rundown apartment in a shady part of North Vegas. I looked at all of the lights and people in disgust as we rode down South Las Vegas Boulevard. The hustle and bustle of the city that never sleeps didn't impress me like it did the first time I was there. As a grown woman almost nine years later, I knew the evil and hurt that laid just beyond the lights. I knew that the saying everything that glitters ain't gold was true because I had lived it. That beautiful city I had ran to with high hopes had chewed me up and spit me out, but I was back for my revenge.

I snapped out of my daze and pulled to the curb in front of a rundown little white apartment building on Coolidge Avenue as Cassie ran down the plan. As I listened to her talk I realized she had went over that plan a thousand times in her mind. She knew what she wanted to happen when she begged for my help, she just needed me to agree.

"So, we are gonna go in. We have to be careful because my dad knows all of the foreign fucks that live in the apartments downstairs and he tells them to watch me. We have to sneak past them and once inside I'll go to my room, get the money, and then we can go. Nothing should slow us down, but if my dad comes home Jess it won't be good. I hope that he doesn't come." Cassie said as she began to wring her hands.

I smirked at her as that rage inside of me started to grow and I reached into the hidden compartment behind my passenger seat and took out my Kel-Tech PMR-30 round .22 magnum pistol, my Big Foot Bowie knife, and the 8-piece portable Field Butcher kit with Scabbard I kept under the seat. I glanced up to see excitement and a hint of fear in Cassie's eyes as I calmly took rubber gloves, a tight plastic cap, and black beanie out of the glove compartment. I slowly and methodically put the plastic cap on my head, tucking my hair inside and covering it with the beanie. I said nothing as I put on the plastic gloves ensuring they were snug on my hands before turning to Cassie. She smirked at me before nodding and jumping out of the car with me trailing close behind her. When we got up to the building we slipped around the back without alerting the two foreign fucks as Cassie called them, who were sitting on the porch downstairs. We snuck up the back stair well without making a sound as the loud voices of people speaking in foreign languages could be heard all around us. My heart raced in my chest as we stopped in front of Cassie's apartment door, and she quickly unlocked it before we slipped inside.

Once inside Cassie went straight to her room as I stood there shocked, looking around at the horrible living conditions. The three-bedroom apartment was filthy with dishes, trash, and clothes everywhere. I held my handgun in my hand with the safety off watching the door as I backed down the hallway behind Cassie. When I made it to her bedroom door I had just stepped my foot inside when I heard the front door fly open.

"Cassie you little bitch! I know you're in here!" Cassie's father yelled from the front door.

I crept inside of the room and quickly, but quietly closed and locked the door behind me. Once inside I put my gun on safety and ordered Cassie to get under the bed.

"He'll kill you." Cassie whispered to me with tears flowing down her face as I pushed her under the bed.

She had no idea what I was capable of, especially in my mind state. I had trained for the exact situation dozens of times, and I was sure my skills would not fail me when I needed them most.

"I'll be okay, just be quiet and stay where you are. When it's over I'll call you out." I said to Cassie calmly as I stood up.

I could hear her father in the front part of the house raging and throwing things around as he searched for her. I put my handgun back into the holster around my waist before walking over to the window and quietly opening it. My heart raced as I let the window up high enough to give the illusion Cassie had went out of it. I froze with my hand still on the window as her father turned the doorknob, discovering it was locked. I quickly wrapped myself in the long, thick purple curtains that were pushed back at the window just as Cassie's dad broke down the door. My hands shook as my adrenaline surged and I reached down to take out my hunting knife holding it up to my chin.

"Cassie, little bitch I'm gonna beat the hell out of you when I find ya!" Her dad yelled as he tore through her room throwing clothes and raggedy pieces of furniture around.

I just wanted to jump out and end his rant as he continued to tear up the room. I stifled the rage inside and held my breath as a roach that was in the curtain ran down my arm. It took everything in me not to yell out and run as the huge insect crawled down my arm, on to my hand, then back on the curtain. I breathed a quiet sigh of relief as the roach disappeared and I focused on the sound of Cassie's father's advancing footsteps. I had to press the butt of the knife to my lips to silence my rage as the maniac dad walked over to the window and looked out.

"Cassie you think I'm stupid. I know your scary ass wouldn't jump out of the window." The man yelled as he turned around and Cassie made a noise under the bed.

I knew right then I had to act. I couldn't let him get his hands on Cassie and unleash the hate he had inside. Just as he lunged towards the bed to pull Cassie out, I unwrapped myself from the curtain with my knife in hand and hate in my heart, beginning the first of my many deadly assaults on my journey to my reunion with Abaddon.

In that instant I think I lost my mind as I rushed forward, grabbing Cassie's dad in a headlock, and pressing the sharp end of my knife up against his throat. He reeked of cheap liquor and cigarettes as his short, thin, 150-pound frame swayed underneath my grip.

"Be still muthafucka! Cassie come out now!" I yelled as the man cursed and swayed in my arms.

I tightened my grip around her dad's neck, sticking my knife deeper into his flesh and breaking skin as he tried to resist.

"Who the fuck are you little bitch? I'm going to kill both of you sluts as soon as I get a loose!" The drunk, irate man yelled as Cassie slid from underneath the bed.

I glanced over to look at Cassie for one second as she got up on her knees and her evil, vicious father kicked her in the face with his steel toed boot. At that same time he flung his head back with all of his might and head-butted me directly in the nose before the impact of the blow knocked me backwards. Blood squirted out of my noise like a fountain, and I felt as if I would black out from the lick's power as I slid down the wall to the floor. Within seconds he was out of my grip and dragging Cassie to her feet by her hair as he turned to look at me in surprise.

"Well lookey here, a nigger. What the fuck Cassie, now you're hanging with filthy monkeys? I tell ya what, how about I see if you monkeys really are nasty whores after I beat your ass once and for all?" Cassie's dad said as I stood up, shaking off my daze and grabbing my knife up off the floor.

Suddenly I felt a strength and insane rage I had never felt before. I stared at Cassie's dad as he stood there laughing and I didn't see him. I saw Abaddon standing there with his cold, dark eyes taunting me. I saw the opportunity I had been waiting for in which I would exact my revenge and kill the demons that stalked me. Without warning I rushed forward quickly, hitting Cassie's father in the throat with the butt end of my knife and kneeing him in the groin at the same time. That perfect combination caused him to let Cassie go quickly and she fell to the floor, crawling over to my feet. Cassie's dad fell to his knees in front of me and before he could react, I hit him in his temple with a jab and kneed him in the face repeatedly. I moved so fast and methodically you would have thought I was a trained assassin from birth. I dazed the drunk, angry man quickly with my barrage of strikes, but he didn't stop fighting. He reached up and tried to choke me as I struggled to stay on my feet. Although drunk, Cassie's dad was pretty strong, and his rage made it no better. He was really giving me a run for my money as I struggled to keep my head up and he yanked on my hair trying to pull me to him as he cursed. That's when I decided I wouldn't try to wrestle with any of my other victims like I was doing with him. That situation quickly taught me that I had to stay in control and get right to business gaining and maintaining the upper hand. I had to make sure I was never in that type of situation again or I would never get my revenge. Instead I would be left abused and broken as a victim once just like before.

"You can never be a victim again, kill him Jess." This faint, eerie voice in my head said to me as I glanced over at Cassie.

In that moment everything around me slowed down as I watched Cassie mouth the words, "Kill Him!"

I felt the butterflies in my stomach rise to my throat as I yanked my hair out of the drunk man's hands and punched him repeatedly with the butt of the knife again. Blood splattered all over my face from the man's nose and he yelled out in anger as I gripped a handful of his hair. My hands shook as I yanked his hair straight up and gripped my knife in my other hand. I could feel all of the hairs all over my body stand up as that faint, eerie voice in my mind spoke again encouraging me to cut his fucking head off.

"Do it Jess, do it NOW! He deserves it and more. He's just like Abaddon. You can't let him get away Jess. KILL HIM!!" the voice yelled over and over again as I swallowed the lump in my throat.

The time had finally come for me to bring revenge to the abused and misused and I stood there shaking, unsure if I could do it.

"Do it for A'Miracle Jess. She could be next." the voice in my head said, hitting my soft spot.

Before I could even think or care about what I was doing I pressed the hooked end of the knife into his jugular and tugged with all of my might. His already abused and thin skin burst open like a piñata at a kids' party as I yanked my knife all the way across the base of his neck. He squirmed in my grip as he gurgled blood while I stuck my knife in deeper. I pressed bit and dug deep into his flesh until I hit bone. After that I pulled my knife out and blood squirted all over Cassie and the dirty, hardwood floor. She growled out in anger as tears ran down her face before she got up on her knees and snatched the knife from my hands. I looked down in her hurt, once terrified eyes and I saw strength and determination as she looked back at me. I saw the will to live and rid herself of demons flicker in Cassie's eyes as she stuck my knife deep into the upper left side of her father's chest while I held his body up by his hair.

"I hate you Richard. I hate you just as much as you hate me. You made my life hell. Now it's time I send you there. I hate youuu!" Cassie cried as she leaned her body weight on the knife and cut a long deep gash into his chest from one side to the bottom side of the other.

Blood flowed from his neck and chest as I continued to hold his body up while Cassie cried and yanked my knife out of his dead body. She cried from that place within that never heals as she held my knife in her hands. As she did that, Cassie talked about all of the horrible things her father had done to her and how he had ruined her life. She vented and sobbed as she let the hurt go and finally found her strength. I could see it in her eyes too as she suddenly stood up with blood all over her and tears streaming down her face.

"We have to go. I'm sure those foreign fucks downstairs heard all of this." Cassie said, suddenly calm and collected as I let her father's hair go and his body dropped to the floor.

I snapped out of the daze I was in where I was imagining myself doing the same thing to Abaddon, just as footsteps and chatter made its way up the back stairs. I looked at Cassie as she backed towards the front door keeping her eyes locked on the back. I watched it too as well as her while I admired the natural survivor instincts she had. Cassie was cool and rational as she slowly opened the front door while men banged on the back. I held my gun in the air and aimed it at the back door with one hand as I grabbed the Glock 17 Generation 4 which was still on my waist and tossed it over to her. On instinct just like I thought, she caught it without hesitation, released the safety, and cocked it. I watched as she moved backwards out of the door like a trained soldier while her eyes danced all around her. I dashed over to the small kitchen and turned on the burners of the gas stove as the foreign fucks continued to bang on the door. I heard them yelling in a foreign language as I backed towards the front door with my gun in hand. As soon as I stepped in the doorway someone kicked the back door open and it flew off it's hinges into the kitchen. Before it could hit the ground I let off six rounds hitting the first three men advancing towards me. I saw that the target practice I had started taking with my best friend Kellen had paid off as I made two head shots and one straight to the heart. I didn't even wait to see their bodies drop before I backed out on to the porch as Cassie went down the steps.

Once I was on the landing and saw that behind me was clear, I turned around to the front. Just as I did, a loud, Arab looking dude appeared at the bottom of the stairs with his gun in hand. He yelled out Cassie's name and then called for help before she riddled his body with bullets from the Glock 17. Cassie hit him fast and hard before she continued down the stairs, crouched down low and focused. I knew right then she wasn't a normal girl and she had been trained in self defense. She was just the type of girl I needed to get closer to Abaddon; someone abused but not broken. I knew that's exactly who Cassie was as she took out another dude who ran out of a door downstairs and I picked off two as they rushed up the walkway.

We dropped their asses like flies without a second thought as I went down the steps behind Cassie. I got down one step before I felt the hair on the back of my neck stand up and felt a gust of wind on my back. My heart raced but I remained calm as I held my gun over my shoulder at an angle. I held my breath and steadied my hand just as someone jumped off the roof and met the bullet I let off. I hit whoever it was as they yelled out and I reached my free hand back over my shoulder. I intended to grab whoever it was in the collar and flip them over my shoulder and down the steps like I had learned in self defense classes. This person was much shorter than I anticipated though so when I reached back I grabbed a handful of long hair. I thought it was a girl, so I turned around ready to fight as I met the punch of a young, short male. The little shit colored, bloody fucker hit me so hard I almost stumbled backwards down the steps. I was able to regain my composure by grabbing the railing as I held him in the hair and then kneed him in the face. Blood poured from his nose and mouth as well as the wound I had put in his neck. He yelled at me in his language as I gained my balance and began to drag him face down, down the concert steps. Blood continued to pour from his face as I drug him to the bottom, dropped him face down on the concrete and then put a bullet in the back of his head.

"Get to the car!" I yelled to Cassie over her gunfire.

I jogged to the car behind her as we picked off everything that moved. Once inside my car I crunk up and prepared to pull off before I stopped to look at all of the carriage we were leaving behind. Bodies were everywhere in the small complex and blood splattered the walls and the once colorful concrete paths. It looked just like a scene from a Stephen King's movie all gory and bleak. All of the death all around us resembled that hell I had lived in which is why I felt no remorse as I sped off. I didn't regret ridding the world of Cassie's abusive, racist father or the foreign fucks who tried to defend him. I didn't care about any of that. All I wanted to do was protect Cassie and other kids like her. I wanted to protect my daughter and ensure no other girl had to go through what I had gone through.

I saw myself in Cassie as she growled in her sleep, and I sped back towards the I-15 headed out of Vegas to regroup and formulate a plan. I wanted to use Cassie's help to get closer to Abaddon so that I could send her on her way. She looked tired, and not just physically as she laid her head on my window and sighed. I saw tears run down the side of her face as her body shuddered and shook. I knew that she was reliving everything that had happened and coming to terms with what she had done. The first kill was always the hardest, so I gave her time. I cut on the radio as I did 90 down the interstate while A Change Is Gonna Come by Sam Cooke came on as I let the soft melody take me. I felt change was about to come as soon as I got my hands-on Abaddon. I would give him a taste of his own medicine and inflict pain he never knew. That was all I could think about as I drove about 240 miles North of Vegas into the city of Ely. I quickly found a Motel 6 off the highway and pulled into the parking lot. After I parked at the edge of the front lot, I looked over at Cassie as she continued to sleep, and I grabbed a towel from under my seat. I wiped the blood from my skin as I thought about how close I was to Abaddon. I could feel him near as I looked at myself in the rearview mirror. I saw a familiar fire in my eyes as I glared at my reflection and thoughts of revenge ran through my head. I could hear Abaddon begging for mercy as I sat there in a daze and bit my bottom lip.

"Jessica. Jessica are you okay?" Cassie suddenly asked me to break my daze as I looked over into her face.

Her eyes had a peaceful glow to them as she asked me if I was alright.

"Yes, I'm fine Cassie. I was just thinking about what I came here to do. Will you help me? And after that I will send you to your mom." I said as she nodded her head and said she would do whatever she could to help me.

"Whatever you need from me I'll give, after all you did for me. I owe you my life." Cassie said before she leaned over and hugged me as I rubbed her back.

As I held her in my arms I just wanted to love on that broken little girl who reminded me so much of the girl I once was. I had to fight back my tears as I let Cassie go and went into the motel to get us a room. After securing the room and key I drove around to the back of the motel and parked my car by the dumpster before we climbed the stairs to our room. I turned back and looked at the brand-new Camaro Justin had just bought me before I opened the door for Cassie and made a mental note to get a new car.

After helping Cassie get rid of her daddy and having his neighbors intervene, I knew that I had to use a bit more decorum in my kills. I had to be sneaky and deceptive like Abaddon was, preying on my victims before I ended their lives. That meant I couldn't be riding around killing pedophiles in something that my husband had bought me. A car that was in my name. That's why once we were inside I sat on the bed and grabbed the telephone book to look for the nearest used car lot and storage facility. I quickly found one of both less than three miles away and got up to make the trip.

"Where are you going Jessica? You're not going to leave me now are you?" Cassie asked as she laid on the bed across from me and stared into my face.

I saw a peace in her eyes she didn't have when we met as I stared down at her and told her my plan.

"I need you to ride with me to get another car and drive mine to storage. You can drive right?" I asked as I grabbed my keys back up off the nightstand and Cassie jumped out of the bed.

She smiled at me as she walked over and grabbed the keys out of my hand before she walked to the door.

"I've been stealing cars and shooting since I was twelve Ms. Jessica." Cassie said as she opened the door and I followed her out.

If her shooting was any indication of her ability to drive, I knew I was in good hands. That's why I said nothing as she ran to the driver's side of my car and hopped in. I just smiled as I got in the passenger seat and Cassie crunk up. She pulled out of the motel lot like a pro as I gave her directions. Cassie got us to the used car lot in five minutes and thirty minutes later I was following her out of the lot as I whipped a used, black 2006 Maximum. Cassie led me to the storage place five minutes away and then she got out of my Camaro and jumped into the passenger seat of the Maximum. She listened to the music I had blasting through the speakers of the old car as I transferred my bags into the used car's trunk and then I parked mine in the storage unit and locked it up. Once it was secure I got back in the car with Cassie and drove back towards the motel. We stopped to get food and snacks for the night and then went back to the room. Back inside Cassie and I ate and talked all about our lives before she went to shower, and I got to work. I retrieved my bag from the trunk and then climbed back in bed before I pulled my laptop and folders out. I thumbed through the red folder of texts that Makayla's friend Ariana had given me as Cassie's beautiful voice from the shower filled my ears. I smiled as I read the texts and something in one of them stood out to me. It was a screenshot of Mikayla's boyfriend's page that showed groups he was in. I read through the short list before I noticed one that said, *Vegas Teens Looking for Friends*. I quickly logged into my fake Facebook account after that only to see that it was a private group.

"Shit!" I said out loud frustrated as Cassie walked out of the bathroom and asked me what was wrong.

She plopped down on the bed beside me as I explained to her what the folders held and the problem I had.

"See, I need a way in this group to get close to Jabari. I just know it's Tony or someone working with him, and I have to find this girl." I told Cassie as she nodded her head and took the computer from my lap.

I sat there and just stared at her as she typed away at the keyboard before she asked me if I was on a fake page.

"Yes, I've had it for a few years, well it and others, but they're strictly for catfish stalking purposes." I said as we both laughed, and Cassie said it was perfect.

She then asked me to take a few pictures of her before she ran back to the bathroom. I knew right then what she intended to do so I jumped up and fixed a place on her bed. By the time she came out of the bathroom with makeup on, a short dress and her hair flowing all around her face I was ready and focused. I gave her a quick photo shoot before we sat back on my bed and Cassie uploaded the pictures. After that she requested to join the group and we sat back. We hadn't even been sitting there ten minutes before Cassie was accepted as Emily and she made an introductory post. In the post she stated she was seventeen, new to Vegas and on her own. She wrote that she was looking for friends and people should inbox her before she attached a pretty picture in which she looked like a child prostitute.

"That should do it Jessica. Just let me know what you need next. I have to take a nap right now." Cassie said as she got up off of my bed and fell into hers.

No sooner than her body hit the unusually soft mattress than she was sound asleep. I smiled as I got up off the bed and covered her up with thoughts of my own daughter racing through my mind. I missed my baby and my husband a lot, so I grabbed my phone and went into the bathroom to make a call. I closed the door and sat on the toilet before I pushed the icon of Justin's handsome face. I felt all safe and warm like I always did when he was around as I stared at his green eyes. I got so lost in his love that I didn't even hear him say hello. I heard nothing he said until he finally yelled my name.

"Jess. Jess, you are playing on the phone now?" Justin asked playfully as I heard A'Miracle laugh in the background and ask if he was talking to me.

"Yes, it is mommy princess. What do you need to say?" Justin asked as I heard A'Miracle's giggles get closer before her excited voice echoed into the phone.

"I love and miss you mommy. Have fun but hurry up and come home!" A'Miracle said as she laughed, and Justin tickled her while he asked if he wasn't enough.

"Of course, you are daddy. I love you. I love my mommy too though. Hurry and come home mommy. Daddy burns the toast." She yelled as I heard Justin try to cover her mouth.

They laughed and wrestled as tears ran from my eyes and I wished I was home. I missed them and their love, but I knew what I was doing was for the greater good. That's why I fought back my tears as Justin got back on to the phone and I told him to tell my baby that I loved her too. She squealed after I said I would be home soon then I heard her leave Justin, so we could talk.

"She's super excited you'll be home soon and even more hype that your dad will be here Thursday." Justin said as I asked him what he meant.

He told me that my dad had called and said he would be in town for the next month.

"You know he has to see A'Miracle, and since you're gone I suggested he stay here with us. You know he agreed to that. Now I'm looking forward to our visit. He even offered to watch the little princess rug rat this weekend, so I can go fishing with the guys. You know I love when your Dad's in town." Justin said as I imagined his smiling, mischievous face.

He and my dad had grown to be best friends over the years and I loved the relationship they had. That's why I was glad my dad would be there to keep Justin occupied while I handled what needed to be done. I knew without that distraction Justin would sense my intentions and stop me before I began. Lucky for me he was more excited than A'Miracle was and didn't even pick up on the vibes I was giving. He accepted the bullshit story I gave him about the first day of my trip before I told him I loved him and would talk to him the next day.

"I love you too Mrs. Michaels now enjoy yourself before I have to come give you a spanking." Justin joked before I purred and told him that I was ready to be punished.

He teased me with talks of our love making before I said that I loved him again and we hung up. I felt lighter and more determined to fulfill my plan after I spoke with my family. I wanted that joy I heard in their voices and the love I got from them to last forever. I knew I had to get rid of Abaddon forever in order for that to happen. That's all I thought about as I left the bathroom and got clothes from my bag to shower. I peeked at the computer to see if Cassie had gotten a bite from Jabari before I sighed and headed to the bathroom. He hadn't responded yet, so I showered and let the hot water wash my worries away. When I got out of the shower I got dressed and then I hopped in the bed as Cassie slept peacefully next to me. It was a quarter until midnight as I sifted through my case files and waited on Jabari to step into my trap. I fell asleep right there in that spot with papers laid across my chest and the computer still on beside my head.

The ping of a notification coming in woke me up at six the next morning as I sat up in the bed. I reached for the computer to find that it was gone, then I looked over to where Cassie had slept. She sat Indian style in bed with earphones in as she typed and bobbed her head to music. When she saw me, she took the earphones out and told me exactly what I wanted to hear.

"He messaged me back a few minutes ago and said he really wants to meet me. I didn't want to wake you up, so I've just been talking to him and building his trust while you slept. It's working too because he just told me to meet him tonight on the strip and he would take care of me. He keeps calling me beautiful and saying he can be my knight in shining armor. My flesh keeps crawling just reading his messages. He's a real fucking creep. I'm going to enjoy helping you with this." Cassie said as I smiled and felt a fire inside of me ignite.

I was finally close to ending my pain and sending those who had hurt me to hell.

"Here I come Abaddon. Here comes your special girl." I whispered out loud as I got out of bed and prepared to take us back to Vegas.

The entire ride back to The City of Sin all I could do was think about how many sins I planned to do there. I could hear Tony's voice in my mind as he yelled at me the night he gave me to the devil, calling me a dirty little rich slut. He had changed from that loving man who only wanted to help into a vicious predator in minutes. I could still feel the pain from his blows to my face and the sting of his words although it was nearly nine years later. That's why I gripped the steering wheel tightly as I drove closer to Vegas and relived my past in my mind. My wounds were still so fresh I could feel Tony's death grip on my wrists as he drug me out of bed. I relived all of the internal anguish and turmoil I had felt that night that Tony and Mark revealed who they really were to me and Quintika before they handed us over to the devil.

As if the memory was etched in stone, I could still see the panic and fear in her eyes as everything went down.

******

I swallowed hard to clear the lump in my throat as I snapped out of my trip down memory lane. When I looked over at Cassie she smiled at me warmly before she reached over to wipe my tears away. I didn't even realize I was crying until I felt her brush the warm liquid off my cheeks.

"What's wrong Jess?" she asked as I pushed the Maximum to 80 miles per hour getting closer to the city as I shook my head and lied.

I told her it was nothing, but I was sure she could see it all over my face. I saw it myself as I glanced in the review mirror and saw my best friend's eyes. I hadn't thought about Quintinka for years because that was a pain I preferred to bury deep. I still carried around the hurt of losing her and the guilt I felt for leading her to Vegas in the first.

I secretly felt that her and Tommy's deaths were all my fault. I felt guilty that me, Justin, and Maria made it out of the clutches of the devil and they didn't. That's why anytime she crossed my mind I couldn't hide my pain. That time was no different as tears continued to fall from my face while I bit my bottom lip.

"I lied Cassie - something is wrong. That something is the fact Abaddon is still alive. I lost my best friend because of him. The world lost a beautiful soul. It was all my fault she died like that and for that reason Abaddon has to pay. Everything he loves must be destroyed. I won't rest until that happens. I don't think I could rest anyway. Even if I wanted to." I told her as a heaviness developed in my heart while I felt my hands begin to shake.

I turned back to the road and drove without thought as my emotions and memories surged. Suddenly as I drove I found myself trapped in a vivid flashback in which I was locked in Abaddon's room. Everything looked exactly as I remembered it. The room even had the same dead, rotten scent covered by the sweet aroma of fresh flowers. Everything was exactly the way it was back when I was a kid kept prisoner behind those walls. I could even hear the classical music he played when he wanted me to dance blast in my ears as I plied on bloody feet across the hardwood floor. I twirled and jumped through the air gracefully feeling free like I did every time I danced. That feeling of free, contentment didn't last long though because suddenly I could feel prying eyes on my back. My blood boiled as my heart raced and Abaddon began a slow clap from behind me.

"That's my girl. You'll be Abaddon's girl forever. No matter how far you run Jess or what you do… it will always lead you back to me. I know how to make you come home and surrender to my will." Abaddon said before he walked his thin, evil, handsome ass into the room piercing my heart with his deep dark eyes.

He looked at me and gave me an evil smirk as he walked over to his bed. I continued to dance on rhythm to the music as I watched him pull out the torture box. Blood and urine dripped from between the slabs of wood as he pulled the box to the middle of the floor. I felt my heart beat in my throat as I watched the box and a pair of bloody hands suddenly appeared from between the bats.

"Please. Let me go. What are you going to do to me? Helllppp!" the girl yelled as her shrill scream surged through me and caused me to spin faster in small circles.

I tried to drown out her cries and pleas for help as Abaddon unlocked the box. As soon as he did, I stopped spinning when I saw the young black girl pop out. It was Mikayla and she was naked, bruised, beaten, and bloody from head to toe.

"Let me go muthafucka!" she yelled as she jumped out of the box with her hands up like claws as she lashed out at Abaddon's face.

She got a chance to put one long slice down his left cheek before he back handed her on to the bed. I stood there frozen in fear as I watched him beat her face until blood poured from her nose and mouth. I shivered as he threw her unconscious body back into the box.

"Yeah, this one a fighter just like you and like Quintika once was. She just doesn't know fighter get it worse. I guess I have to teach her then. Or you could help me and step into the First Lady role I gave you long ago. The choice is yours My Jess, Abaddon's girl." He said as I shivered in fear.

"In the meantime, though. You two can bond." Abaddon said as he walked over to me and snatched me up by the hair.

He gave me a chop across the throat fast as he drug me over to the little box and threw me in on top of Mikayla.

"Remember you're mine Jess. You and our child. You can't escape me even in your dreams because I always get what I want. I'll always be in your mind Jess. As well as in that tight little pussy and your heart too. So just stop fighting it and come on home. You better snap out of this daydream and make a decision quick though because Mikayla won't last much longer! Come on home Abaddon's girl. Come find me!" His evil voice said in my daydream, and I snapped out of it just as Cassie yelled.

I looked up to see that I was drifting to the side of the road and was about to hit the Welcome to Las Vegas sign.

"You okay Jessica? I know you didn't get much sleep. You want me to drive?" Cassie asked as I shook my head no while I pulled us safely back on to the road.

I swallowed back my memories and the deep pain I still carried inside as I told her all I wanted was for it to be over with.

"He has her Cassie. I can feel it. I have to find her fast." I said as anxiety and rage took over me and I punched the gas petal to the floor.

"Let's go get these bastards then. I'm with you Jess." Cassie said as we rode back into Vegas and found a room.

I chose the Tropicana Las Vegas hotel right on the strip near the Hard Rock Cafe and used my fake ID and credit card to secure our stay. I wanted it to be like I wasn't even in Vegas, so I could get the information I needed and go. I was on a mission with no time to waste after having that dream about Mikayla with Abaddon. That's why once we were settled into the beautiful suite and had showered, Cassie and I got straight to business. She spent most of the day inboxing and Face timing Jabari, getting him ready for our trap. I sat by the table near the door and cleaned my guns, anticipating what was to come. I could just feel that Jabari was the key to Tony and that would lead me to Abaddon. So, I set up a fool proof plan to catch him up after Cassie said that he was in the same hotel.

"Okay, you say they're on the first floor, that's perfect for us. That will make our get away easy after we do what must be done." I said as Cassie agreed, and I asked her for the room number.

As she strolled through her messages with Jabari to find the room number I got up from the table and walked over to my bag. I grabbed two costume wigs I had brought along with me and threw one to Cassie before I slipped my blonde one on.

"Room 119. He said it's right by an exit and the employee elevator that leads to the basement." Cassie said as she sat the laptop on the bed and grabbed the red wig I had thrown to her and slipped it on.

We both stood in the mirror side by side and adjusted our wigs as I thanked her for her help.

"No thanks needed Jess. You saved my life. Now let's go save Mikayla." Cassie said with conviction as she walked to the door, and I grabbed us both a Ruger Silent-SR .22 handgun from my bag.

Cassie and I quickly secured our guns before we left our room on the fifth floor and headed to the elevators. In seconds we were on the first floor and headed towards room 119. When we got on the back hall the room was in I felt butterflies in my stomach and heart and a lump formed in my throat. The hair on my arms and the back of my neck stood up was we walked the hall right past the room. I could hear the TV blasting behind the door and the thick pungent smell of cigar smoke filled my nose as I nodded at Cassie then looked at the emergency exit at the end of the hall and employee elevator directly next door. It was close enough for someone to transport girls discreetly without anyone seeing. I knew that was what it was used for too as we walked towards the ice machine next to the exit and the door to room 119 suddenly swung open.

"Yeah Mark, I got three lined up for today. Two are on their way to meet me now and I get one tonight. She's a pretty little blonde too. I bet Tony will be happy because that tight little ass will bring in top dollar." the tall, dark, model looking brother whom I recognized as Jabari from the screenshots Arianna had given me, said as he closed the room door and looked our way.

I grabbed Cassie in my arms and pretended to kiss her as Jabari looked at us. I kept her face hidden as I ran my fingers through the back of her wig and turned my head from side to side like I was in a deep kiss.

"Ohhhhh. I came out at the right time. Fuck those three I got two right here." I heard Jabari say as I continued to fake kiss Cassie and Mark yelled back at him from the phone.

He asked Jabari what it was and after he told him, Mark yelled for him to move on.

"Okay, okay you're right. We have more important shit to do. You bitches come to room 119 though if you want to add some more chocolate to that swirl. Hell, I got nuts too." he said before I finally glared over Cassie's shoulder at him and looked right into his eyes.

I could tell he saw the hate and malice in me although he was five feet away. He stood frozen for a second before he smirked and walked away. I watched him as he talked to Mark all the way down the hall then disappear into the hotel.

"He definitely knows where Mikayla is. That was Mark on the phone with him. Now I just need you to follow the plan." I told Cassie as she said she was on it before she walked to the end of the hall.

Like planned she watched for Jabari as I pulled a miniature remote listening device out of my pocket that was attached to a small retractable wire. I turned it on and then kneeled to slip it under the door. I was able to secure it to the baseboard right next to the door jam before I pulled out the wire and stood up. After that I nodded at Cassie before I put the master key to the elevator I pulled from my pocket into the elevator slot and it opened.

"I'll be right back. Text me if he comes." I said before Cassie nodded and I stepped inside.

My heart raced as I went one floor down to the basement and the elevator opened to the loading dock. It was just like I thought, they were using the elevator to get kids they had captive out of the hotel. The scratches on the door next to the elevator and drops of blood on the concrete loading dock let me know my suspicions were true. I wondered how many poor kids were trafficked out of that exit as I went back upstairs and met Cassie.

"That's how they get them out. Now I have to figure out our exit." I whispered to her from the end of the hall before she nodded and told me to hurry up.

After that I held my breath as I pushed the emergency door open expecting an alarm to go off. I looked at Cassie shocked when it didn't then I stuck my head out of the door and looked up. I saw that the wires for the door alarm had been cut already making that a discrete exit and entrance. I knew what I would do then as I closed the door and met Cassie at the end of the hall.

"This should be easy. Those bastards won't know what hit them." I told her before we went back to the elevator and once we were on, we took off our wigs.

Back in our room, Cassie and I packed up our things then she showered and got ready for her date while I took the things to the car and parked it around back. It was a little after six when she finished her hair and makeup then joined me back in the room.

"You look beautiful Cassie. Now just remember what we planned. Kick it with him at the Hard Rock and get him to like you so he'll invite you back to the room. I know he will anyway because his plan is to ship you off tonight. He won't get a chance to do that though because I'll be right there. I'll be listening in on everything too. That's what this is for." I told her as I got up and clipped two butterfly pins into the front of her hair. "Walk into the bathroom and say something." I told her before I stepped out into the hallway with my earphones in my ear.

Suddenly her voice came through loud and clear as she said she was ready to go.

"Let's get it then." I said satisfied as I opened the door back up and Cassie walked out.

After that she and I talked about the plan a little more before she got into the elevator. As soon as she stepped in her phone rang and she said it was Jabari.

"He must be there waiting on me. It's show time." Cassie said as she squealed.

I told her I would be watching before she nodded and answered the phone. She said hello just as the elevator doors closed and she disappeared. I stood there by the elevator and paced for about ten minutes once Cassie was gone, listening to her conversation with Jabari. She had put him on speaker as she walked down the strip and he wooed her like Tony had done me.

"Every since I saw your picture Emily, you have been on my mind. I can't wait to wrap my arms around you and hold you tight. I'm going to treat you like a queen. Hurry up and get here. I can't wait anymore." Jabari said in this fake, smooth tone as Cassie giggled like a naïve schoolgirl.

She was so convincing as she laughed and told him that would be her dream. She damn near had me fooled when she told him she just wanted to be loved. I knew it was some truth to that due to her upbringing, but she said it with so much emphasis it damn near sounded real. Jabari thought so too as he ate her words up and told Cassie that was what he liked to hear.

"I bet you do sick bastard." I said as the elevator doors opened, and a fat white man looked at me crazy.

I gave him a fake smile before I stepped into the elevator beside him, headed to Cassie. I continued to listen as I walked the strip feeling less excited than I had when I walked the same path nine years before. Quintinka and I had been so mesmerized by the bright lights of the city when we walked we didn't see the evil that lurked. I saw it that time though as I glared at sex trafficking scouters posted up everywhere. I was able to pick them out the crowd fawning on all the naïve, innocent girls on the strip. I wanted to stop and kill a few as I walked by but I knew I had something more important to do. That's why I just continued to the Hard Rock and found me a booth by the door as I watched Cassie and Jabari at the bar.

Using the same Knight in Shining Armor M.O. that Tony and Mark used, Jabari wined and dined Cassie all night. He fed her then bought out the bar offering her one drink after the next. I saw her turn down a few, but when he grew a little suspicious she began to drink. Cassie still maintained her power though knowing she had to be alert for what would come next. By the time 11 rolled around she had

Jabari right where we wanted him, drunk and caught off guard. He didn't even think twice about inviting her to the room which she quickly accepted. I got up and left then so I could beat them back to the room. I did that too and had just stepped through the door of the emergency exit to wait when I heard a familiar voice come down the hall.

"So, you know the rules for disobeying. Now you must be punished." Mark's voice said as I peeked out the window on the door and saw him pushing a young girl down the hall by her neck.

She appeared to be about fifteen and was wearing a really short dress with long weave in her head. Mascara streaks ran down her face as she cried and told Mark she would get more money.

"Nah, fuck that. You had your chance. You're getting shipped out to New York tonight. No more easy life living in the hotel and meeting dates. Your ass about to be locked down. But not before I remind you what happens when you disobey." Mark said as he opened the door and then hit the girl so hard that she flew in the room.

I could hear her body hit the ground before she screamed, and Mark closed the door. I grabbed the knob and pulled my gun out ready to kill him right then, but I heard voices coming down the hall. I ducked back inside just as Cassie and Jabari casually walked towards the room. He swayed slightly, clearly drunk as Cassie held him up.

"Maybe we should do this another time." Cassie said testing him as they stood at the door, and he struggled to get his key out of his pocket.

I knew Cassie was just stalling him to see if I was in place, so I peeked my head in front of the window. I held up two fingers to let her know someone was already in the room then she nodded as Jabari opened up the door. I could still hear Mark raging in the room as Jabari pushed Cassie inside.

"Don't get scared now my snowflake. You belong to me. Ain't no leaving once you in, so go ahead and take a seat." Jabari said as the door closed, and he locked Cassie inside.

I could hear her breathe rapidly through the device as she did what he said. After that I listened as he began to discuss the arrangement with Mark.

"This the snow bunny I was telling you about. You owe me $8,000 for her and the one from last night. She's downstairs tied up where I left her, thinking about what she did. I can guarantee by the time you get her upstate she'll be ready to comply. I did good, didn't I?" Jabari asked as Mark laughed and told him he had done good.

"This a nice little piece, but what she is working with under these clothes?" I heard Mark ask as Cassie's breathing picked up and I could tell she was getting mad.

I could hear the rage she suppressed as she pulled clothing over her head past the wire in her hair. She took a few deep breaths as she asked them what they were going to do with her. From the way they oohed and smacked their lips, it was easy to assess what was on their minds. I felt confident Cassie was ready for that too as I heard her chuckle under her breath. We had discussed her possibly having to get naked or touched on so that we could get Jabari comfortable to catch him off guard. I hadn't planned on Mark being there when I made that plan but knowing that he was there made Cassie's sacrifice even more important. We needed one of them weakened so that I would be able to creep in. Cassie must have sensed that too because she suddenly began to fake cry before she said she would take off her clothes.

"Yeah take them ALL off and let my nigga Jabari get a sample. He spent all his money on you tonight, so you owe him anyway." Mark said.

I felt enraged as I listened to his sick ass while I imagined Cassie getting naked in front of them. I could barely keep myself behind that door as I heard Jabari moan as he touched on her.

"Yeah, that body soft baby. Come on up here and lay on top of me." He told her as I heard the bed shift and Mark said he was ready for the show.

After that I heard him order the girl he had with him up on to the bed then her screams filled my ears. I could hear him smack her as he raped her while Cassie's breathing picked up. Soon the sounds of snoring overpowered the girls screams and I knew Jabari was out. The eye drops I had given Cassie to put in his drink had worked right in the nick of time. That's why I moved fast as I put the ski mask I had in my pocket on my face, cocked my gun and ran out the door. I tip toed over to room 119 and stuck the key I had stolen from the front desk into the slot. I heard no movement after it opened, so I rushed in ready for war. When I did Cassie popped up like a Jack in the Box as she grabbed Jabari's gun from the nightstand while Mark upped his. He was still laying on the bed beneath the bloody girl as he held his gun and peered at me over her shoulder.

"Who the fuck are you bitch? And what the fuck are you doing in here?!" Mark yelled as he pointed his gun at me while Cassie inched across the bed.

I took my mask off as Mark kept his eyes on me while he threw the girl off him and onto the floor. As he did that Cassie got closer to him without drawing any attention to herself. He didn't even notice her creep up on the side of the bed and stick her gun to his head because he was looking at me so intensely.

"Hold up. Don't I know you? I've seen your face before." he said as I inched closer giving him a better view of my face.

He realized Cassie was there then, so he slowly lowered his gun while he continued to look into my eyes. I gave him an evil smile before I let off one shot from my silencer that pierced the skin right above his groin. Mark screamed out in agony as blood squirted all over the thick white comforter on the bed and Cassie covered his mouth with her free hand.

"Jessica!" he mumbled surprised from beneath Cassie's hands as he squirmed.

I laughed that same sadistic, eerie laugh Abaddon used as I walked up to the bed.

"Yes, it's me you nasty evil bastard and you already know what I'm here for. I see you bastards are still up to your old tricks." I said as I glanced around the room at all of the Coach and Fendi bags sprawled everywhere.

I knew then that they had coaxed those girls in the same way he and Tony did me and Quintika. I said that too as tears welled in my eyes and my hands began to shake.

"Yes, I remember you now. Little country Jess and her girl Quintika. You're the little rich bitch who got away. Why the fuck is you back?!" he yelled as I reached over and smacked him across the mouth with my gun and blood splattered all over me.

I hit him a few more times across the head with all of my might before I stood back and laughed.

"I'm back to give you a taste of your own medicine you freak. I want you to see how it feels to lose someone close to you. Jabari's your little homie huh? He's the dumb lost soul you have leading helpless girls into your grasp? He's helping you satisfy Abaddon's sick needs, huh? That's what he does?" I asked irate as I shook, and I watched Mark's eyes get big.

I could tell he knew shit wouldn't end well for him as tears began to pour from his eyes.

"He's my brother-in-law. Please. He's just a kid. He doesn't understand." Mark begged as I laughed and ordered Cassie to get dressed.

"Put on your clothes so we can show this fucker how it feels to lose someone you love." I said as I held my gun in his face and Cassie quickly got dressed.

Once she was done she scurried over to the bed and pressed Jabari's gun into the back of his unconscious head.

"Wake up you sexy, evil bastard. It's time to play." Cassie said as she poked Jabari in the head with the gun and then smacked him with it, but he didn't move.

I watched her as she checked for his pulse after that then turned back to me as she laughed.

"Looks like he's already dead. I guess I gave him too many drops." Cassie said as she shrugged, and Mark cried like a baby.

He bawled and squirmed in the bed as I grabbed a towel off the nightstand and stuck it in his mouth.

"Shut the fuck up. You're crying like a little bitch. Those tears mean nothing to me though, just like ours meant nothing to you. Hold this bastard down. I got something for him. Something that will ensure he never hurts another girl again." I said to Cassie as she rushed over and straddled Mark's bloody body, pinning his arms beneath her knees.

I put my gun up and pulled my hunting knife with the serrated edges out of my pocket and walked to the end of the bed. As I walked I suddenly heard a whisper from behind me. I turned to see the girl still on the floor as she stared over at us with wide eyes.

"You can go. Get out of here and don't tell anyone what you saw." I told the girl as she cried and said she had to see him die.

I understood that need as I turned back to Mark, and he squirmed beneath Cassie's weight.

"You are a pedophile Mark. A sexual predator and you deserve to die. I'll give you one chance to save your miserable life. Just tell me where Tony and Abaddon are." I lied as I heard him grunt and he tried to push Cassie off.

I saw he needed a little encouragement, so I sat my knife down and quickly ripped off his pants. I picked my knife back up and grabbed his limp dick in my palm as I yelled out my question again.

"Where are they punta? Tell me now or we're playing dice with your balls tonight." I said in an irate tone as Cassie pulled the towel from his mouth then Mark begged me to stop.

"Okay, Okay, I don't know where Abaddon is, but I can give you Tony's address. Just don't do it." he said.

I laughed as I squeezed his small, pink dick in my hand, and he screamed out for me to look in his phone. The girl jumped up then and grabbed it off the nightstand before he rambled off the lock code. In seconds she was in the phone and had found the text Mark said was there.

"See it has the address to the house we were taking the shipment to in New York. You have everything you need to find him. Now let me go." Mark said as I looked at the girl and she nodded her head.

She flashed the phone at me and I saw the Bronx address and phone number in a text. That was all I needed.

"Okay, I will let you go now. I'll let you go straight to hell." I said as I grabbed his dick in my hand tightly again and without thinking, I began to cut it from his body.

I cut so deep and so close to his balls I was able to pull his whole scrotum out. Blood splattered all through the air and Mark screamed behind Cassie's hand as I held his dick and balls in my palm.

"Now choke on this shit you pussy. Choke all the way to hell." I said as I walked to the head of the bed and Cassie moved her hands.

Mark's mouth was wide open as he screamed, and I stuck his dick and balls down his throat. I stuck it as far as I could with my hand then I used the end of my knife to stick it further down and lodge it in his windpipe. After that I watched as his eyes got big and his body began to twitch while he grabbed at his throat. He gagged and foamed at the mouth as Cassie jumped up and we looked down at Mark's pitiful ass.

"Revenge is so sweet. Don't worry love, Tony and Abaddon are next." I whispered in his ear before I kissed his forehead and left him there to choke to death.

The girl handed me the phone before her and Cassie followed me to the door then we turned to look back at him. I watched as he flapped around for a second then suddenly his body went limp.

"Good reddens." The girl said as I opened the door.

"You two go. I'll handle this. After all, I was the victim. I'm sure once they find the girls in the basement, I won't go to jail. You two just disappear. I got everything else." she said as I wasted no time breaking for the exit.

Once I got through the door with Cassie on my tail I heard the girl yell out thank you before she began to scream. I had no time to respond as I led Cassie to the car, and we hopped in before I sped away.

"One down and two to go." I said as I drove out the hotel parking lot headed back to New York City to end my hell once and for all.

I couldn't help but to feel guilty as I jumped back on the I-15 headed out of Vegas while Cassie sighed from the passenger seat. I felt no remorse for what I did to Mark or any of the others, but I did feel bad for what I was doing to Cassie. I said that I was helping her, at least that's what I told myself. However, in reality I knew what I was doing was for my own selfish reasons. I wanted to get those men who caused me pain much more than I wanted to save her. That's why I hadn't seen the effects of what we we're doing until I stared over into her face. Cassie had deep wrinkle lines in her pale skin and huge bags under her eyes. Her seventeen-year-old face had changed into that of a thirty-year-old woman in a matter of days. I took responsibility for that although I knew her troubles started long before she met me. That still didn't ease my heart though as I watched her move restlessly in her seat, so I had to speak up.

"You know I appreciate your help in all of this Cassie, but I think it's time we part ways. I really hate I ever brought you into this, and for that I'm sorry. I can take you to the first bus station that I pass on my way to New York and get you to your mom in Minnesota. I'm sorry for all of this though, and I hope you can forgive me. I was selfish bringing you in to this. What I did was no better than what Jabari and Mark were doing." I said as I drove on looking straight ahead as Cassie sat up in her seat.

I heard her clear her throat before she turned slightly towards me.

"Jess don't say that. What you did was the most selfless thing anyone has done for me my whole life. You saved me from a man who was bent on breaking me down. You helped me find my inner strength, and for that I will always be grateful. It's not selfish of you to want to rid yourself of the man who hurt you most. You did the same for me. You deserve this relief too." she said before I suddenly looked at her like she had lost her mind.

To me it didn't look like she had gained relief after all the blood we had shed. It appeared to me that she was coming apart at the seams, but she quickly told me I was wrong.

"Don't think because I'm sitting her quiet, I'm feeling remorseful or regretting something because I'm not. I'd do it all again in a heartbeat. I was just sitting her thinking about what we'll do to Tony when we find him. I think he deserves something special, so I was trying to figure out the perfect torture. You already neutered Mark, so I don't know how we can top that." Cassie said as she thought out loud and I glanced over at her.

I still felt bad from the guilt I carried but I couldn't help but to laugh when she suggested impalement.

"It would be pedophile on a stick. A real horn dog special." Cassie said as we laughed and drove towards our next destination.

I planned to send her home as soon as my revenge on Tony was done. In the meantime, though I drove on auto pilot trapped in my memories and thoughts of revenge. Cassie chattered as the radio played and I made my way up I-15 on a numbing seven-hour drive only stopping to pee, get food, and stretch.

It was about 7:30 that next morning when I entered the city of Evanston, Wyoming and the car began to putter and jerk beneath me. I looked over to see Cassie was fast asleep as a beeping sound filled my ears.

"What the hell?" I said out loud to myself as I looked at the dash to see the check engine light had come on.

"Damn, it's just my luck." I said out loud to myself as I passed a sign for gas, food, and lodging then took the exit and found a shop.

It was right beside a motel that had a confederate flag hanging outside and a huge statue of a ram by the door. I slowed down the car and looked around as the black girl in me woke up. There I was in red neck country with a beat up little white girl, running after committing multiple murders. It didn't matter that I was the daughter of a music mogul with more money in my trust than the town was worth. I knew all that they would see was the color of my skin and I would be lynched before I had a chance to talk. That's why I woke Cassie up after I parked by the door and sent her inside to go get us a room. She came back as I strolled through my phone and then texted Justin to tell him I would call soon.

"You did right not to go in there Jess. I felt like I was in a scene from Rosewood." Cassie replied as the rebel within me awakened and I joked about going to shoot the place up. "We should be from this looks of this place, we'd probably be killing the whole city population." Cassie said as I laughed and backed up to drive over to the room.

I laughed but I felt like she was right when a fat, red neck with a beer in hand walked out of the hotel dragging a little girl by her hand behind him. He glared at me with pure disgust as I smiled and waved back at him.

"That's the last thing I need right now, so just keep it moving Stone Cold. I'll stick that can up your fat ass." I said out of the window as the fat man gasped and Cassie laughed while I wondered what was happening to me.

Meek, soft spoken Jess who had escaped hell and then went on to live a prominent life in LA was long gone and had been replaced by the female version of Abaddon himself. I didn't act, think, or feel like myself anymore. My rage and need for revenge had consumed me so much I felt like a guest in my own body. I hadn't even recognized myself since I left home headed for Vegas. I was losing, myself to hate and I hated it, but I knew it was necessary. I tried to shake off my thoughts as I drove to the back of the hotel and parked in front of our room.

After grabbing my bag, me and Cassie got out and went inside as the fat white man and his daughter walked up. They went right into the room next door to us before I slammed the door shut. I could hear him yelling at the child through the wall as I plopped down on the bed.

"I really hope I don't have to kill a racist piece of shit before we leave Wyoming. I'm tired man." I said as I fell back on the bed and covered my face with my eyes.

Cassie told me to get some sleep before she asked what time the shop opened.

"The website said eight. We can go over there after I catch a few winks." I told her before she said she would take the car over and for me to just try to rest.

"I know a lot about cars. I could probably fix it myself if I had the right parts. That's the only useful things my worthless ass father ever taught me my whole life. I guess it will come in handy now so thank you rotten ass dad." Cassie said as she looked down at the floor then laughed nervously.

I knew she was struggling with her feelings then, so I smiled warmly at her before she walked towards the door.

"I'll be back as soon as I find out what's wrong. Sleep Jess. It's a lot of road between here and New York. I'll bring breakfast back with me." Cassie said as she opened the door, and I threw her the keys.

As soon as she was gone I pulled my phone out of my pocket and called my husband. I needed to talk to Justin right then to feel his love and remember the loving person I was really was. Just in delivered too when he answered the phone in pure Romeo fashion.

"Why hello my gorgeous, Nubian queen. It's s good to hear your voice." Justin said as my heart melted, and I swallowed back some tears.

I told him how much I missed him as I hid the anguish I felt inside.

"We miss you too baby. Isn't that right princess rug rats?" Justin asked A'Miracle as she said yes in a groggy tone.

Justin then went on to tell me she had slept with him because she said he was lonely without me. I smiled as I wiped tears from my eyes and my husband babbled about his day. I felt the love I needed as we got deep in conversation and by the time we were about to get off the phone I felt like my old self. That is until Justin told me about a dream he had.

"It was weird as hell because we were at some farmhouse out in the country, fighting Abaddon." He whispered, and I could hear a familiar rage in his tone.

"Like you told me baby, you just have to get it out of your mind. The nine-year anniversary of our escape is coming up. That's the reason for your dream. Don't worry I'll be home soon. Like in about a week and when I get there I'll wipe all of your worry away." I said trying to divert his attention away from that subject altogether.

I didn't want Justin getting his magical intuition and figuring out what I was up too. That's why I told him I was going to fuck him to sleep when I got home then suck him until he woke back up.

"Now that's something to look forward to. Something that will erase any bad dream. Hurry up and get your sexy ass home Mrs. Michaels." Justin said as I told him it would be sooner than he thought then we said our I loves and hung up.

I laid there still feeling his love as I fell into a deep sleep.

Several hours later I woke up to the sounds of a little girl screaming. I opened my eyes and peered around the room as the yells of the fat man vibrated the walls

"I PAID GOOD MONEY FOR YOU. NOW DO WHAT YOU'RE TOLD!" he yelled to the little girl as she screamed, and something hard bounced off the wall.

I jumped up and grabbed my bag after I heard that and pulled out my gun with the silencer. I walked to the door ready to end the man's miserable life, just as Cassie stormed in.

"Jess, good you're awoke. The car is fixed. Once we finish breakfast we can hit the rode." she said as she walked in past me with cups and bags in her hand.

She didn't notice I was standing there with my gun until she got to the table and sat the food down.

"What? What's going on?" Cassie asked confused as the screams and yelling picked up again.

She sucked her teeth and picked the phone back up as she gave me a knowing glance. We said nothing to each other as she grabbed the food, and I got my bag. We walked outside and threw the things in the car before I turned to Cassie and spoke.

"How did you get the car fixed with no money?" I asked her as I checked my ammo and then cocked my gun.

She told me she had done a hard job for the mechanic and in return he gave her the parts for our car.

"Some things just take a woman's touch. He learned that lesson today. Now it's time we teach this fat fuck the same thing." I told Cassie as she nodded and pulled her gun from her waistband.

After that we walked to the room door and waited as the man continued to rage inside. I nodded at Cassie as she checked her gun then I stepped beside the door. When I did she stepped forward and knocked before it quickly swung open. The man reached out and grabbed Cassie quickly by the throat as she let off shots into the room and the girl screamed. I rushed around the corner into the room as the man slammed Cassie into the floor.

"Little bitch. What do you want? You came to give me some pussy too. I'm not paying for you. You're a bonus fuck you scraggly little whore! Come here!" he yelled before he lifted his foot to kick Cassie and I let off a shot into his back.

I hit him right in one of his huge rolls as he suddenly froze. I expected him to fall as blood trickled down his back, but he growled and turned around instead. He lunged all 300 of his pounds straight towards me as I squeezed the trigger. My shot missed him, and my gun fell to the floor as he slapped me across the face with his massive hand then grabbed a handful of my hair.

"Well look here. It's the smart mouth nigger. Another bonus for me. I get to break me a coon." he said as he tried to man handle me by slinging me around by my hair.

He didn't count on me being used to that type of physical torture after being in Abaddon's grasp. That's why I was able to block out the pain as I gained my balance and reached into the pocket of my pants. As he hit me and tried to throw me to the floor, I managed to get my blade out. I swung upwards with it, using force and drove my knife right threw his chin.

"Arrgghh." The man yelled as blood poured from his mouth and chin.

He held the bottom of my knife handle and staggered backwards as he looked in my eyes. I smirked at him seeing Abaddon's face instead of his as I ran forward towards him at full speed. I did an elegant kick that contained nothing but power and sent him tumbling back to the ground. As soon as his body hit the floor I was on him faster than a lion on its pretty. I grabbed my bloody knife handle and with all of my might, I snatched the knife out. Blood shot up in my face like a water hose as the man moaned and gurgled blood while he tried to hold his wounds. He looked up at me with wide terrified eyes and I saw nothing but the beast who had hurt me. I saw Abaddon's prying evil eyes at that moment and lost my mind. Cassie's hands on my shoulders and the little girls screams snapped me out of my rage. I looked down at the bloody, mangled face of the man as I snatched my knife out of his flesh.

"It's over Jess. That nasty bastard is chopped meat now." Cassie said as she pulled me up and the little girl crept towards the man's body.

I stood beside Cassie as we both watched the girl, excepting her to be upset. I knew that a lot of victims sympathized with their abuser, so I thought the girl would cry. She didn't though she just stood over the man and looked down at his corpse. She blinked rapidly as she twirled her finger in her strawberry curls and bit her bottom lip. Then suddenly she reached down and slipped her tiny hand in the man's pocket and pulled a necklace out. Cassie and I watched as she kissed it then told the man she hoped he would go to hell.

"He hurt daddy; and I heard my mama crying before he took me away. He can never hurt me again now, can he?" she said as tears suddenly fell from her eyes.

My mama lion intuition took over me then as I walked over and swooped her up into my arms before I told her that her nightmare was over.

"That bad man will never hurt you again. I promise you that. And I'm going to get you back to your mommy." I told her before she wrapped her arms around my neck and laid her head on my chest.

She cried softly as I stroked her hair and Cassie searched the room. She found a brief case with pictures and video tapes of sexual acts being performed on kids. There was even catalogs with pictures of kids pedophiles could buy like a new pair of shoes.

"This sick bastard had a whole kiddy, sex tape ring. Nasty bastard." Cassie said before she walked over and kicked the man in the head.

She said she wished we could have made him suffer more as I wished the same. I was happy we had stopped him from hurting the little girl though and all I wanted to see was her back with her mom. That's why after I told Cassie to check outside and she said it was all clear I put the little girl down

"I know you have been through a lot baby, but right now I need you to be a big girl. We're going to give you some food and sit you on the steps outside. By the time you finish eating someone will be here to take you to your mommy. You never have to see the bad man again. You're safe now." I told her as I looked down into her big blue eyes then wiped her tears away.

She sucked up her breath and nodded her head before me and her walked out of the room.

"Clean up anything we touched." I told Cassie as I ran to the car and grabbed the food she had bought.

I got both bags and cups before I ran back over to the little girl and told her to follow me to the steps. I sat her down with the food as she watched my face intently then asked me my name.

"My name is Quintika." I told her using my best friend's name because I felt she was my angel.

I knew that Quintika watched over me just like I had done the girl. That's why I told her that then rubbed her hair before I said I had to go.

"My name is Caroline. Thank you, Ms. Quintika." the girl said with tears in her eyes as I choked back tears of my own.

I had to run away from her and back to the car to keep from grabbing her and never letting go. I wanted to wait and make sure she was taken care of but I knew I couldn't do that. That's why I just got into the car as tears fell from my eyes and Cassie came out of the room. She jumped in the passenger seat and told me to pull off because she had called the cops.

"We can watch from the hill behind here. I saw it when I went to get the car fixed. We can go there and watch if you want, but we have to go." she said as I wasted no time pulling out of the parking lot.

I took Cassie's directions to the hill behind the hotel and parked where I could see. Less than five minutes after we had parked, I watched as the cops and ambulance pulled up. I got out and looked on as they went straight to the girl and made sure she was okay. After that I watched as they went into the room and discovered the gory scene and evidence inside. I heard them yell out they had found the man they were looking for before I got back into the car. Once inside a dozen emotions hit me at once as I cried and punched the steering wheel.

"What the fuck am I doing? I'm not God. I can't decide who lives and dies. I'm no better than them." I said as I cried from deep inside of me while Cassie rubbed my back

"No Jess, you're a hero. You've saved two girls. Because of you they are alive. As a matter of fact, you saved four including yourself and Maria. I know you never imagined doing the things we've done but look at the results Jess. Look down there." she said as she pointed down the hill and I stared at the smiling little girl in a woman cop's arms.

"Look at that baby Jessica. Without you she would be dead. I would be dead Jess. You're doing what God wants you to do. You're saving people and ridding the world of devils in the flesh. Why else do you think he led us here? It's six other hotels on this street. We could have gone anywhere but he led us here, so you could save that girl. You're better than them Jess. You're better than most people. Because of you she will sleep in a bed at home tonight instead of being a concubine for some old pervert. This is your calling Jess. This what he wants us to do." Cassie said as I soaked up her words and felt it in my soul.

My tears of sorrow turned into tears of joy as I watched another cop car pull up. Suddenly a short white woman with strawberry blonde hair jumped out and limped over to Caroline as she cried. I watched as the little girl was reunited with her mother and I felt I was doing what I was supposed to do. If my quest to my revenge on Abaddon meant a few extra bodies along the way, I was ready for it.

"You're right Cassie. If we don't protect these kids who will. You're wise beyond your years and I'm glad you're here. I'm still sending you home soon but for now let's go! Let's get the fuck out of here and see what else this highway to hell holds." I told Cassie before I crunk up and we jumped on I-80 headed to New York.

We left there determined to find Tony and save any other tortured souls we came across along the way.

I rode I-80 for hours trapped in my thoughts before Cassie took the wheel. Once she did I got into the passenger seat and tried to hide my pain. I was in internal turmoil over the things I was doing. Although part of me knew it all was for the best, the innocent sweet Jess within me couldn't help but to weep. I never imagined I would be out killing and torturing people the same way Abaddon had done me. It didn't matter that they were horrible people who caused nothing but pain in the world, they were still human beings. I was still human too beyond the nightmares and anxiety as well as the scars and my emotional pain. I still had a desire to see love and hope in others, which is why I felt so bad. I closed my eyes and settled into the seat as Cassie turned the radio on and India Arie's song 'Beautiful' blast through the speakers. I closed my eyes and swayed to the music and I suddenly saw myself dressed in elegant dance gear as I plied through a field of roses with Cassie, A'Miracle, and Mikayla by my side.

I fell into a deep dream after that in which happiness and love enveloped me. I saw the world like I always wanted it to be, peaceful and quiet. I found that wasn't true sometime later though when Cassie's irate voice filled my ears. I open my eyes and sat up in my seat before I looked around to see it was the next day. Cassie had driven through the night, getting us further across the country closer to New York. I saw a sign that said Elkwood, Illinois next to the gas station we were parked in front of. Right in front of the car was Cassie standing with her hands on her hips as she argued with another young white girl with red hair. The girl had the gas pump in her hand as Cassie yanked it from her grasp. I watched her as she back handed the girl and then returned the pump to its holder. Stunned and not about the life Cassie was, the girl held her face as she walked back to her car. Cassie pulled out her gun as she stood by the pump and watched the girl pull off.

After that she casually walked back towards the car as she noticed me watching her. Her eyes got big as she quickly put her gun away and hopped back into the car. I just glared at the side of her head as I wondered what type of monster I had created. I realized at that moment she was just like me, and I had changed her like Abaddon had done me. He had awakened a beast in me that I felt I could no longer contain. I saw that same hate and animal thirst in Cassie's eyes as she looked over at me and tried to laugh it off.

"These country ass people crazy and rude for no reason. That Heifa just cut me off and then thought she was going to pump some gas. She had me messed up though. Good thing she backed off or she would have gotten a bullet to her face. I'm not letting anyone run over me ever again. I'm not weak Cassie anymore. I can thank you for that Jess." Cassie said as I shook my head then looked at my lap feeling guilty as hell.

She was right, it was my fault that she was being reckless and ready to take a life without second thought. I had awakened a part of her that should have been left hidden, and for that I felt I could never forgive myself. I knew that the only way to make it right would be to get Cassie where she belonged. That's why after she pulled up to the pump, turned off the car, and prepared to get out, I grabbed her arm to stop her.

"Cassie, I'm sorry. I'm sorry for all of this. We can't be out here just killing people though. That's not what my mission is about. I hate I brought you into this shit, but I know how to make it right." I said before I got out of the car and walked around it as Cassie got out too.

She asked me what I had to do as I handed her money and told her to go pay for the gas. She glared at me suspiciously as she slowly walked away, and I got into the driver's seat. I watched her until she put her hand on the gas station door handle before I crunk up and began to pull off. I hated to leave her out in the middle of nowhere but in my heart, I felt it was right. I didn't want that little girl following me across the country anymore and further damaging her already fragile soul. That's why as she ran after the car I continued to drive as tears fell from my eyes.

"Wait Jess. Noooo. Don't leave me now. I need you just as much as you need me. I'll listen and do what you say. Just don't leave me when I need you the most. Please Jess. I'll die if you go now!" Cassie yelled as she ran behind the car and her words tugged at my heart.

I looked back at her in the rearview mirror just as I was about to pull out of the lot, and I couldn't help but to stop. I knew that she was right. I did need her. She probably needed me too which is why she didn't want to let go. I put my head down on the steering wheel and cried as Cassie jumped back into the car. She cried too as she hugged my back and apologized for her actions.

"I'm sorry Jess I know I overreacted back there, and I know that my recklessness could have gotten us caught. I'm just tired and hungry so I blew up. Please forgive me but don't leave me. I'm not ready to go home yet. I'm not ready to face the reality that awaits me there. Don't make me go. I can help you Jess. I don't have to kill I can just be a decoy. What we're doing is saving lives Jess. Don't take this away from me. This is the most good I've done for others in my entire life. Don't take this Jess please. Just let me help you." Cassie begged as I looked up at her and nodded my head.

I crunk back up the car and backed back up to the pump before I turned the engine off. I still felt guilty for having Cassie involved and I still planned to send her home. I just knew I had to do it easier to keep from putting more bruises on her heart. I saw the pain of a girl who had been abused and deserted all of her life in Cassie's eyes as she looked over and thanked me.

"I promise Jess, I'll just be here to help. Just don't make me go back now." Cassie said as she sniffled, and I reached over and wrapped her in my arms.

She told me it was more to her story that she hadn't said, and I felt it in her touch. I didn't want to send her back knowing she wasn't ready to go. She felt safe with me and I felt better knowing someone was around. That's why I told her that we were good, and I was going to make sure she got the rest that she needed.

"Get out and pump the gas you crazy, little, white chocolate, mini me." I said once I had let her go and we laughed as we got out.

I went in and paid for the gas while Cassie pumped and when I got back in the car we left. We found a Mc Donald's and Motel 6 less than half a mile down the road, so we got food and a room then went inside to relax. Once we ate Cassie and I showered then fell asleep before our heads hit the pillows. I fell right into a vivid nightmare too. A reoccurring one that I couldn't escape. I was trapped in a room with Abaddon again as he made me dance while he watched with his prying eyes. Mikayla and Cassie hung from the walls on hooks like some weird, human life art piece. I could hear their moans and screams over the classical music that played as I plied for my life. Suddenly A'Miracle appeared in a pink butterfly tutu with a dog collar around her neck. Blood stained the front of her bodysuit and there were scratches all over her face. She cried as Abaddon's evil voice boomed through the air while he demanded that she dance. I watched blood pour from her feet as she got up on her bruised little toes while she sobbed and begged me to help her.

"Mama please. Make the bad man stop. He hurts me." she cried as Abaddon wrapped her up in his arms and she squirmed and cried in fear.

I screamed too as I tried to run over to them but suddenly I felt glued to the floor. I couldn't move as I cried out for the devil to let my baby go.

"OUR BABY. Remember that Jess. She belongs to US. I'll have her in my arms soon. I'll have you too." Abaddon said as he held A'Miracle close to his chest and ran his hands through her hair.

He coaxed her like a loving dad for a second then he reached down and smacked her so hard that her teeth chattered as she screamed.

"Mommmyyyy help me!" A' Miracle yelled as I jumped straight up out of my dream.

Sweat poured from my head as I sat up in the bed and glanced over at a sleeping Cassie. The sun which had just come up shined through the curtains at the window and illuminated her face. The light gave her a beautiful glow that made her look like an angel. That made me think of my own pretty little princess angel and the terrible dream I had. I quickly reached over to the nightstand and grabbed my phone before I pushed Justin's icon and called home. I had been gone three days at that point and I missed them both very much. I needed to feel their love at that moment and know that my baby was okay. My dreams were so vivid that they felt real, so I had to be sure. That's why I jumped out of bed and paced as Justin's phone went straight to voicemail. It was Monday morning and although he had gone on a trip, I felt he should have been back home. I felt panic rush over me as I dialed my home phone and it rung until the answering machine came on. When it did I left a message telling Justin to call me.

"Baby I'm trying not to be frantic but you not answering the phone for me is not helping. I need to know you all are alright. So, Justin, CALL ME! I love you two." I said just as our answering machine beeped and the phone hung up.

I felt worry rush over me as I stood there holding the phone and Cassie woke up.

"What's wrong Jess?" Cassie asked me as she sat up in bed and I walked over and plopped down beside her.

I quickly told her about my dream and how Justin wasn't answering the phone for me.

"Its just all in your mind Jess. Just like you told Justin. That anniversary is weighing heavy on you too. You gotta relax. Once we get to New York, get Tony, and get the jump on Abaddon you'll feel better. In the meantime, though you gotta stay calm. Justin and A'Miracle are okay. You said your dad was in town. Maybe they went out? Two men alone with plenty money. Jess, I can guarantee they're having fun. Trust me. Okay?" Cassie said as I pushed my anxiety to the back of my mind.

I wanted to believe what she said was true but something inside me said something wasn't right. I had no proof just anxiety and worry, two things I knew that would do me no good. That's why I got up from the bed, showered and emerged from the bathroom a different Jess. I was back on track and ready to finish what I had started although my family was on my mind. I planned to make a trip back home to make sure they were okay after I got Tony. Making that plan in my mind soothed my nerves enough that I was able to move on with my day. After Cassie showered and dressed, we checked out before we stopped for food and got back on the road.

I hopped on to I-90 and drove until my eyes got tired. It was about eight that Monday evening when Cassie and I passed the sign welcoming us to New York. After 34 hours of driving, over 2,000 miles, and a half dozen of bodies, we had finally made it to our destination. My heart raced in my chest as we went through the toll booth then headed to Brooklyn. Although I was tired I didn't want to waste any time getting down to business. I drove in a daze as I relived my last time in New York in my mind. I remembered riding over that bridge on my way back home with my parents after being released from the hospital and Abaddon's grasp. I remembered how I felt relieved but scared knowing that things still weren't over. I knew that without Abaddon in custody, I'd have to face that demon again some day. I was right too as chills ran through me and we entered Brooklyn and went to the address Mark had given us. I felt my throat tighten up and the air leave my lungs when we pulled up in front of this big brown building. It looked just like the hell I had been trapped in with its metal doors and no windows in sight. I grabbed the phone and checked the address before I told Cassie it was the place. We looked around the busy street as a tall, slim Jamaican man came out of the house next to the building. He swayed slightly like he was drunk as he smiled and walked around the back of the building. I could tell he was a junky, drunk, or homeless man from his disheveled appearance and the yellow tint in his eyes. What I couldn't figure out was how he was related to such upscale crime bosses as Tony and Mark.

Although they were predators, they ran a million-dollar cartel. They dressed like it too with all of their flashy clothes, jewelry and expensive cars. I saw none of that around the warehouse or the rundown house next door. That made me think that Mark had sent me and Cassie on a wild goose chase. I was just about to say that too when something behind the building caught my eye. I saw the tall Jamaican man ushering a little girl through the bushes behind the building and over to the house.

"Look at that." I told Cassie as she peered through the darkness then sucked her teeth. "He's definitely involved with Abaddon and Tony in some type of way. We gotta get to him to find Tony. And help those girls. We can't do this shit alone though. I have to call help." I told Cassie as I drove to the end of the block and backed into the yard of an abandoned house.

As soon as I parked I pulled my phone out of my pocket and called my dad's best friend Chubb. Chubb was my daddy's street connect in New York as well as his best friend. He had helped my daddy when he came to New York to recuse me from Abaddon. That's why I knew he would be game to help me with no questions asked. I was right too because as soon as he answered he asked me what was up.

"My niece the big-time doctor. What did I do to deserve the honor of this call? I been calling your daddy's old jiggalo ass for three days now and he won't answer." Chubb said as my heart raced hearing him say that.

My dad wasn't answering just like Justin wasn't and that worried me. I tried not to let that consume me as I swallowed the lump in my throat and then spoke.

"He's in LA at my house with Justin. I've been trying to call them too. That's not what I'm hitting you up for though Unc. I need your help." I told Chubb and he was all ears as I gave him the rundown.

I told him my intentions before I begged him not to call my dad. "This is something I just have to do Unc. I know you understand. It's girls in this fucking warehouse and they have Mikayla somewhere." I said as my uncle told me no explanation was even necessary.

"You just stay put niece. I'm mobilizing the soldiers now. We've had about fifteen girls who have gone missing in Brooklyn this past month. I bet that's where they are. We're going to get them back. I got you niece, shoot me the address and I'll be there within the hour." Chubb said before I thanked him and hung up the phone.

After that I texted him the address then Cassie and I sat back to wait. We kept our eyes on the front door of the house as well as the perimeter of the warehouse for about 45 minutes before I pulled our wigs and ski mask out of my bag, ready to go in. I got a text from my uncle saying they were in route and three minutes away as I put on my wig and told Cassie to do the same. I didn't want anyone seeing us and recognizing our faces, so we wouldn't be linked to the other murders. Once we had our wigs secured we got out of the car as my uncle pulled down the block three vans deep. They pulled up with their lights off before my uncle parked at the curb in front of me. The other two vans parked down the block and then goons in all black jumped out. I walked to the curb with Cassie on my tail as my uncle got out and asked me the plan.

"We go in this house and save the little girl he has before we question the nigga. Send some of your goons over to that warehouse and have them post up all around it. When we hit this house have them hit the building and lay every grown man in there down. I'm sure it's some girls trapped in there so make sure they know that too. Tell them to look specifically for a black girl named Mikayla who is about seventeen." I said before my uncle hugged me then got on his phone to do what he did best.

He quickly gave the orders through the phone and we watched as the goons fanned out, taking their positions. Cassie and I slipped our ski masks on as my uncle did the same. He pulled a 12-gauge from his pants leg before he stepped into the street and nodded us across.

Cassie and I stealth across the street and ran around to the back of the house while my uncle held up the rear. When we got to the back door I could hear Marvin Gaye blasting and a loud smacking sound. I looked at Cassie with a disgusted expression on my face as I imagined what that sound was. My heart began to race as a dozen horrible thoughts ran through my mind. I needed to save that girl that's why I reached over and turned the knob to find the door unlocked. I opened it and slowly pushed the door open before my uncle rushed in. He held his 12-gauge tightly ready to slump a nigga as his 350, 6"7 frame moved silently and methodically through the small kitchen. I saw him peek his head into the living room and freeze before he glanced back at me. The look on his face told me that my worst nightmare had come true. I tiptoed beside him with my heart in my throat as I glanced inside and wanted to scream. There the Jamaican junky was sitting on the couch with his back to us and a girl about twelve between his legs. I didn't even give myself time to actually see the nasty shit he had her doing before I rushed inside. I had my gun out ready to knock his head off, but I stopped at the last minute. I needed to keep him alive long enough to get a location on Tony. That's why I put my gun up as I glanced around and spotted the long cable cord laying on the floor. I snatched it up quickly and looped the ends around my hands before I wrapped it around the man's neck. I grabbed him quick and with purpose as I tightened the cord around his throat. As he grabbed at the cord and groaned I put my foot on the back of the couch to push off. I choked the shit out of the man as he flapped around and tried to pull the cord from his neck.

"Stop moving you pervert bastard!" I yelled as my uncle ran over and began to pummel the man.

He hit the gasping man hard and fast with his massive fists as Cassie swooped in to grab the girl. She walked her out of the room as I continued to choke the man while my uncle beat his ass.

"Tell her what she wants to know or you're going to die sick bitch." My uncle said as he hit the man in the temple with a right hook that made his head snap to one side as he moaned.

I just continued to choke for a few more seconds as he gasped for air. I let him go as he tried to take in breath and keep his head up at the same time.

"Tell me where Tony and Abaddon are muthafucka!" I yelled as he moaned.

He wasn't answering my question fast enough, so I pulled my knife out and stuck it to his neck. I pressed it into his skin deep and hard as blood began to trickle from the wound.

"Okay, okay you crazy bitch. I'll tell you where Tony at. I don't know about no fucking Abaddon, you psycho hoe!" The man yelled sounding like one of Abaddon's guards who used to abuse me in his prison.

His words stoked the fire within me and I growled as I grabbed his ear in my hand. I sliced it off and threw it into his lap before he could even finish his rant.

"Can you hear me now you bastard? Tell me where Tony is at?" I yelled over his screams as he held the spot that was once an ear.

"He's in Harlem where he lives. This is just the safe house. I'm here to watch the product before they're sold. That's it." he said as he cried, and I looked down at the top of his head in disgust.

"It seems you're doing much more than watching the product to me muthafucka!" My uncle yelled before he punched the man hard in the gut and he emptied the contents of his stomach.

Vomit shot all over the floor as he moaned, and I asked my question again.

"He's in Harlem I told you. The address is in that phone he gave me. The only reason I have that address where he lives in luxury with the white folks is because I followed him home one day. It's all in there: a map, pictures, and everything else you need to find him. You know all I know; now let me the fuck go. I don't know why you're looking for him anyway because what he has going will never stop."

the bloody, beaten and bruised man said in a distorted voice as he spit out teeth and laughed. "We sell hundreds a week and get new shipments in each day. You shut this warehouse down and another will pop up around the block by tonight. You can't stop what he has going bitch. Why even try? Most of those little muthafuckas ain't gonna be shit anyway. We're doing the world a favor." the man said before he moaned out in pain then let out an evil laugh.

I glared at him with malice before I stabbed him in the back. I dug my knife in just deep enough to make him scream out in pain but not nearly deep enough to kill him. I couldn't believe he was so evil, so I had no problem bringing him pain. I twisted my knife a little in the wound as he cried then I quickly pulled it out. I wiped away the blood that had splattered on my face before I walked over to grab the man's phone while he groaned, and my uncle beat him silly. Once I went through the phone and found all of the information I needed to locate Tony I was done. I was done being remorseful or even caring about the sick muthafuckas we killed. That's why I pulled out my gun as I walked past my uncle right up to the couch and put a bullet in the man's head. I blew his brains out all over the dirty, gray walls and then turned around to leave. As I got to the door my uncle's phone rang and I stopped while he answered it. He talked for a second and then got silent before he hung up.

"What's going on Unc? Was it girls in there? Did they find Mikayla?" I asked him as his face turned red and he couldn't look at me.

I didn't wait on his response then I just ran out the door and off the porch past Cassie and the girl. My uncle yelled my name as he chased me down and grabbed me by my arm.

"Jess stop. Mikayla is not in there. You don't need to see the rest. Come on baby. Let's just go." my uncle said as my heart dropped into my stomach, and I felt like I would throw up.

That didn't stop me from breaking away from him as I ran around the building and through the open door. I ran into a long line of bruised crying boys and girls who were being led out by one of my uncle's goons. Tears fell down my face as I ran past them to the top of a flight of concert steps and stopped. I looked into a familiar dungeon as memories came rushing back to me. I went down the steps with my eyes closed as I remembered the same walk down the steps to hell. When I got to the bottom and my uncle grabbed my hand, I opened my eyes to the horrors my uncle wouldn't speak of.

Dead bodies of girls and guards killed by my uncle's goons were sprawled all over the floor. Bloody torture devices lay on tables all over the room and cages lined the back wall. I covered my mouth with my hands as I glanced to the back of the room and saw a young boy dead, naked, and strapped in a sex swing with a puddle of blood beneath his body. The scene was so gory and the smell in the dark basement was so strong, I couldn't help but to throw up. I vomited up my stomach lining as I coughed and cried my way back up the steps. I cried for all the children who suffered down there and those who didn't make it out. My tears turned into an angry growl as I emerged from the back of the warehouse with one thing on my mind. It was time to kill the last of the minions and then slay the fucking dragon.

"I gotta find Tony now!" I told my uncle and Cassie once we had returned to the spot where our cars were parked.

The cops were on the way and the girls were safe, so it was time for me to move on. My uncle told me I wasn't making a move without him before he told one of his goons to drive his van and he hopped in with us. I pulled off the block going 90 miles per hour as cop cars raced by.

I raced to Jackie Robinson Parkway headed to Queens as screams and images flashed in my mind. I was so anxious to get my hands-on Tony and make him feel the same pain Mark had felt, my hands shook on the steering wheel. My uncle saw that from the backseat, so he told me to pull over so he could drive, and I quickly agreed. I got out and took the backseat behind him as he jumped in the driver's seat.

"You just sit back there and relax nieces pieces. I got this. What's the address?" My uncle asked as I sat there numb.

I heard his question, but I couldn't answer because I was so consumed by the rage inside me. Cassie turned and looked at me before she nodded and rambled off the address.

"11033 64th Road." Cassie said."It's in the Forest Hills neighborhood." she told my uncle as he nodded and then jumped on Jackie Robinson Parkway.

"Oh this muthafucka really is out there with the white folks. We can't go get him how we did at that house in Brooklyn. Police will be everywhere after the first shot. We gotta find a way in." my uncle said as he drove, and I listened through my haze.

I had no idea how we would navigate through the affluent neighborhood and get into Tony's home undetected. Cassie knew how though, and she quickly spoke up as I stared out the window.

"I think this key might help us." she said as she held up a shiny gold key that reflected off the window.

The glisten got my attention and I turned to the front as she continued.

"I got this key from the girl at that house. Her name was Kesha and when I took her outside she started telling me all she knew. She said that Tony keeps his money makers, the cute girls, at the house with him out here in Queens. She said she was out there getting pimped out to sick, old white people until about a week ago. She said that's when he discovered she was plotting to leave and sent her back to the warehouse. She said it's five other girls there and from her description, I think one might be Mikayla." Cassie said as she glared at me in the rearview mirror and tears welled in my eyes.

I hoped like hell one of those girls were Mikayla and I'd find her safe. That's all I thought about as Cassie continued talking and my uncle grunted from behind the wheel.

"She said this is the key to the back half of the entire building Tony lives in was one reason she had to go. She said she didn't mind being sent away for refusing to have sex with multiple men at one time. She said she took her ass whooping and left because she knew she had this key. She wanted to kill him herself, but I told her you would handle it for her." Cassie said as she handed the key back to me and I perked up a little.

I felt relieved knowing I had an easy way in and Tony was nearing his death. I held on to that key like it was The Hope Diamond as my uncle and Cassie continued to talk.

"Okay, so we park a block away on 63rd and walk over to get the bastard." My uncle said as Cassie agreed and said it should be easy.

"So how are you doing this Jess? Do I need to load a few more guns?" she asked me as I shook my head no and said that the ones we had should be enough.

"I know this bastard, he flashy. He trying to fit in out here. It will be no need for extra guns. We may be able to get him without a gun at all. There will be no guards because that would indicate he's weak and expose his true lifestyle to his neighbors. He never shows weakness and he's too smart to lose this position, so I can bet my life that he's alone. He's alone with those girls being the pervert he truly is." I said disgusted as I sucked my teeth and tucked the key in my palm.

Twenty-four minutes after my uncle jumped behind the wheel we entered the Forest Hills section of Queens. It was beautiful like my uncle had said with its fancy apartment buildings and clean streets. We rode past one majestic building with a big, elegant red door and my uncle nodded his head at it.

"That's the place right there. We can duck and hide the car right here by this park." My uncle said as he drove past the house as I eyed it as he whipped around the corner.

I reached into my bag on the back seat and grabbed a taser as my uncle backed into a service entrance of the park right up to the gate, and we jumped out. Cassie and I slipped our wigs on and held our masks in our hands as we followed my uncle towards the house. My heart raced as we walked through an area with heavy trees that was connected to the park then stopped at a fence.

"There's the house. Stay close to me once we're over the fence." my uncle Chubb said as he slipped his mask on and me and Cassie followed suit.

Once it was done my uncle hopped over the fence like a true hood nigga and Cassie did the same. I could tell they had been hopping fences for a long time and I knew I had never done it before. I did have the grace of a prima ballerina though, so I utilized my classical dance roots. I ran back a little as my uncle and Cassie stared at me crazy through the fence. I held up my hands before I ran as fast as I could and leaped gracefully over the fence. I landed on my feet and then bowed before them as my uncle shook his head.

"It's still in you baby girl. See that? You're born with that type of grace." my uncle said proudly as he smirked at Cassie then he turned back to me. "That bastard couldn't kill your light baby. All of it is still inside of you. You have to get back to dancing Jess." my uncle said as I shook my head no and he said we would talk about it later.

I nodded in agreement as I eyed the massive building about eight feet away. I didn't have time to think of that dream I had deferred when I was feet away from my nightmare. Killing Tony and getting closer to Abaddon's was much more important. That's why I ignored the anxiety growing inside of me as I looked around the massive yard.

All was quiet and dark with nothing moving so I told them it was clear.

"Let's go." I said to my uncle and Cassie as I held the key between my fingers and made my way to the back door.

I panted, and my hands shook once I made it to the door of the back apartment and slipped the key in the lock. Part of me expected it to be a trick or a trap to catch us off guard. However, when I turned the key and the door unlocked, I knew that Tony was just still dumb as hell. Frivolous and privileged he had gotten caught slipping by s little girl and lost his key. Lucky for me he did because it let us right in. We stealth through the empty, luxurious apartment like ninjas and when we made it to the front door I paused. I knew that anyone with sense who owned an entire apartment building and lived in it like a single-family home would have any unused portions locked off. That's what a sensible person would do, but Tony lacked both morals and common sense. The door was unlocked, and we were able to slip out of it and I to the building with ease. We walked down the hallway single filed as I noticed the other three apartments on that floor didn't have doors. They all were made up like individual rooms in a house instead of 1-bedroom apartments.

"Rich bastard." Cassie mumbled as we made it to the bottom of a winding staircase.

We could hear classical music playing and a shower running upstairs as my uncle pushed me back and began up the stairs. Cassie and I followed him as he held his pump out in front of us. He led the way with that powerful machine as Tony's singing overpowered the music.

"Beautiful girl. You are my world. Beautiful girlll! I'm coming my Kay Kay!" Tony sang as we crept up to his bedroom door.

I felt my body begin to shake as I stepped into the room behind my uncle and Cassie to see it set up just like Abaddon's room once was. There was a huge bed in the middle of the room with floor length mirrors on all of the walls. One side had a ballerina bar set up and a sex swing dangled from the ceiling. I couldn't help but to get trapped in my memories for a second as I stood there and shuddered. I saw myself naked and bruised at the bar dancing for my life. I could feel Abaddon's eyes burning through my skin as I tried to hide my fear. Everything was so vivid; all of the emotions, the smells, and sounds. It was just like the hell which had been my reality for months. Those similarities made me feel like I had never escaped. I was still that abused little girl at heart as I stood there and trembled. Cassie must have seen the internal pain I was going through because as my uncle crept to the open bathroom door, Cassie walked over to me. She grabbed me by my shoulders and called my name until I snapped out of my trance.

"It's okay Jess. He's not here and he can never hurt you again. You're not a victim anymore Jessica. You are the hero. Take back your power. Find that strength you gave me." Cassie said as I stared into her eyes and summoned her strength.

I could feel rage surge through as I heard Justin and Maria's voices in my mind. They told me to kill Tony for us all; those few who lived and the ones who never made it out. That's why despite my trembling legs and the fact that my heart was beating in my throat, I walked forward towards the bathroom door as I pulled my taser out.

"He's deep into his shower. That bastard doesn't even know we're here. Let me take him out now and get this over with." my uncle said as he raised his 12-gauge and pointed it towards Tony behind the glass shower door.

He was ready to shatter the glass and send that fucker to hell. I couldn't let him do that though. Not before I got the information I needed to set Mikayla free and that would lead me to Abaddon. I whispered that to him too as he nodded his head and lowered his gun before I walked past him. I held my Taser tightly in one hand as I grabbed the shower door with the other and held my breath. I could see Tony standing there with his back to me as he continued to sing, and water poured down on him

There he was - the man who had broken my heart and led me to the devil. Just looking at him all happy and carefree while I still lived with the pain sent me into a rage. Without thinking I walked forward and stuck the taser to the center of his back. 10,000 volts of electricity shot through his wet body as he shook and a little surged through me. I dropped the taser as he continued to shake and turned to stare in my face. His eyes got big as he recognized my face while slowly walked towards me. I was frozen in rage as I pulled my knife out and I heard my uncle open the other side of the shower. Tony called my name and walked closer to me as my uncle stepped inside.

"Jessica, you came back." he said as he held out his arms like he was going to embrace me.

He was just about to grab me when my uncle hit him in the back of the head with his 12-gauge. Tony slumped to the shower floor in seconds, and I glared down at him as I growled. Suddenly all of my fear, pain, and anxiety had disappeared. All that was left was an uncontrollable rage and all I wanted was to see him in pain. That's why I yelled for my uncle to get something to tie him up with as Cassie asked me what I wanted her to do.

"Go search his cabinets for an electric mixer and grab some knives and pliers if you see them." I told her as I saw my entire plan I had worked on for years in my mind, finally take shape.

Cassie ran away as my uncle came back into the bathroom from Tony's bedroom with handcuffs in his hand.

"This freaky fetish bastard already had what you need." my uncle said with a disgusted look on his face as he booted Tony up the ass.

"Lucky for us. Lift that bitch up. Hang him from the frame of the shower. I got something special for him." I said to my uncle as he went to work, and I dashed away for the one thing I had forgotten to tell Cassie to get.

I passed her as I ran into the kitchen and opened the pantry.

"What are you looking for Jess? I found the stuff. I have
everything you need right here." Cassie said as she held up the hand
mixer, pliers, and a block full of chef knives.

I nodded my head at her before I turned back to the pantry
shelves and spotted the one thing we were missing. I grabbed the
giant box of salt from the shelf and walked out of the pantry and past
Cassie as she stared. I smirked at her then nodded to indicate she
should follow me to see. I had made it to the bedroom door before she
finally caught on and came running behind me.

"Ohhhh, I get it now. Jess you're on some real torture shit. I'm
all in." Cassie said as she walked into the room behind me, and I
stopped to glare at her from the bathroom door.

She knew that I didn't want her involved with anymore killing so
I didn't even have to say it. Cassie nodded her head before I turned
back around and stepped into the bathroom. She scurried in behind
me and sat down all of my tools as I stared at my uncle. He had
Tony's hands handcuffed over his head across the shower stall frame.
He had been beating the now conscious Tony too as he asked him
where the girls were.

"What girls do you speak of? Nobody's here but me. I don't
know what kind of stories Jess has filled your mind with, but rest
assured that I it's not true. She's just an old girlfriend. A woman
scorned really. Ain't that right Jessica?" Tony asked with that cocky
ass voice as my uncle slapped his ass to sleep.

Chubb hit him so damn hard and so many times in a second,
Tony's head bounced off the stone, shower wall. He was out like a
light and snoring as I stared at my uncle

"Well damn UNC. You incredible hulked his ass. I would have
rather gotten the information first, but that works too. I know how to
wake his bitch ass back up." I said as I grabbed the pliers Cassie had
placed on the counter and walked back over to him.

I got on my tiptoes as I glared at Tony's bruised, bloody face. I
put the pliers on the end of his beautifully manicured index finger of
his right hand and then ripped that bitch off. The sound of the nail

disconnecting from his skin and his screams as he woke up made my ears pop. That didn't stop me from continuing the process as he screamed and spit on me

"You bitch. I'm going to kill you. If I don't Abaddon will. Argghhh!" Tony yelled as I laughed and ripped each one of his fingernails off.

By the time I had finished the last pinky, Tony was a little more inclined to cooperate.

"Okay, okay. It's three girls in the basement. Go through apartment three in the back and look in the bathroom for the hidden door behind the long mirror. They're in there all alone but they're safe." Tony said as he sobbed, and I nodded at Cassie to go see.

She pulled out her gun and cocked it before she ran towards the door. Once at the bathroom door she stopped and turned back to look at Tony.

"The girl said there was five of them, and with her gone that leaves four. Where's the other girl you pervert?" Cassie said as I looked at him and asked the same.

He stared down at me with cold, dark eyes just like Abaddon's as he laughed.

"Beggars can't be choosey. Take what I'm giving you." Tony said before I hit him at the same time my uncle did, and we slumped him again.

Tony snored as his head dangled and I told my uncle to go with Cassie.

"You stay over there away from him until I get back." my uncle Chubb said as I agreed and stepped over to the counter to organize my instruments.

I laid out the knifes and placed the salt beside it before I turned back to Tony. If he only knew the pain that was on the way he would have told me what I wanted to know. I knew there was no chance of that though as he came to and continued to laugh.

"You can't save them all Jess. Nobody saved you." Tony said as he laughed and I grabbed the filet knife up off the counter and walked towards him.

I wanted to slice that smug ass smile right off his face. I probably would have done that too if my uncle didn't suddenly rush back in.

"It's three of them down there. They were tied up and badly beaten." my uncle Chubb said as I stared at him with tears in my eyes and he already knew my question

"No, Mikayla was not one of them Jess. She wasn't there." my uncle said as Tony laughed and asked me if that was who I was looking for.

"My Kay Kay? That's who you came to save? You'll never get her. She's perfect. Like a work of art that should be hung up and admired. You were once that precious Jess. Now you're nothing to me. You'll be another kill for Abaddon though when he catches up to you. He'll always find you Jess, but you won't be finding Mikayla." Tony said as he laughed, and my uncle punched him in the gut.

Tony emptied the contents of his stomach all over the shower floor as I told him he would in fact talk. He saw that I was serious when I began to cut his shirt from his body. I moved calmly and methodically as I talked to my uncle like nothing was going on.

"You got them all free?" I asked as my uncle told me yes and said Cassie had them.

"Cassie's comforting them because one little girl was hysterical. This sick bastard had sewed her eyes shut and she had gashes all over her body." my uncle said with a pained expression before he turned back to Tony enraged. "Where's the other girl muthafucka? And where is Abaddon at?" my uncle asked as he gave Tony nothing but body shots as he groaned and laughed.

Unlike Mark and the Jamaican man, I could see that Tony wouldn't fold. His loyalty to Abaddon's was too deep for that so he just continued to laugh. I screamed in rage knowing I had come so far and still wouldn't get what I wanted.

"You bastard. If I can't get him I'll just kill you then. Not before I make you suffer!" I screamed as I put the filet knife under his arm.

I cut a thin layer of skin from his armpit and then ripped it from his body as he yelled for dear life.

"You gonna tell me now?" I asked as he growled and told me to go to hell. "Not before you do bitch." I said before I cut the skin from under his other arm.

Tony shook in pain and spit as he cried, and I walked back over to the counter. I grabbed the salt before I walked back over to him and rubbed it in his wounds. Tony spit and screamed in agony as he squirmed but he still wouldn't tell me what I wanted to know.

"I'll never tell you bitch, and you will never find Mikayla. You won't find Abaddon either, but believe me, he will find you. He's probably curled up in bed with little A'Miracle right now." Tony said touching that spot in my heart that drove me insane.

Without even thinking I rushed back over to the counter and grabbed a butcher's knife and ran back over to him. I hacked at his skin everywhere the knife touched, and blood and flesh flew through the air. I was out of my mind with hatred t that point, I couldn't even stop. I didn't let up until my uncle grabbed me by the shoulder and told me he was gone. I stared straight ahead at Tony's bloody body and saw what I had done. Every inch of his skin had a deep gash, or a puncture wound from my knife. Piss ran down his leg as he took in a shallow breath but never let it out.

"He's gone Jess." my uncle Chubb said as he hugged me, and I cried angry tears.

I cried about how I had let Mikayla down as a thought suddenly popped in my mind. I knew that from the way Tony talked, Mikayla was his favorite like I was to Abaddon. That meant he kept her close by.

"She's perfect. Like a work of art that should be on a wall." I heard his voice say in my mind and I knew exactly where Mikayla was.

I broke my uncle's embrace and ran into the bedroom as he followed close behind. I stopped right at the foot of the huge bed and glared up at the floor length picture of a naked woman that hung over the bed.

"Like a work of art." I said out loud as my uncle caught my drift.

He quickly put up his gun up and flipped the mattress of the bed then pushed back the frame. I stood there with my heart in my throat as I watched him move the huge, heavy picture. When he finally had it off the wall and, on the floor. I gasped at what I saw. There was Mikayla in the wall behind makeshift bars. She had blood all over her face and the front of her clothes as she cried out for help.

"We're here Mikayla." I said as I sobbed, and she glanced at me wondering how I knew her name.

After that my uncle snatched the bars away with all of his might and lifted Mikayla out of the hole. She cried and thanked him as he sat her down then she asked me how I knew her and where she was at.

"I was once you Mikayla, so I had to come find you. I slayed the dragon too." I said as I stared at the bathroom door.

I saw fire and rage ignite in Mikayla's eyes then as she ran in and screamed. I followed her into the bathroom with my uncle behind me and we stood back as she grabbed a knife and began to stab Tony. She gutted his dead body like a fish as she cried.

"I hate you for all you did to me. I hate you!" she said.

I walked over and grabbed her from behind as I told her it would be alright

"You're safe now and he can never hurt you again. I know hearing it does nothing for the pain and memories, but knowing he's gone will heal some of the wounds." I told her as she dropped the knife and then my uncle quickly scooped it up.

He went around the room and grabbed up or wiped down everything we had touched. I stood next to Mikayla and held her hand as we cried and glared at the man who had ruined our lives.

"I just wish I could have gotten him to talk so I can find Abaddon." I said defeated as I turned and pulled her towards the bedroom.

When she heard that Mikayla suddenly stopped as she told me she may have what I need. She let me go and ran into the bedroom as I followed her slowly inside. I watched her as she unzipped the bottom of the mattress and pulled out a big, brown book out.

"I think this is something like a catalog or pedophile address book. I saw that name Abaddon in here before though." Mikayla said as she flipped through the pages of the book and my heart stopped when she got to the next to the last page. "Here he is right here. He lives in Delaware." Mikayla said as I walked over and grabbed the book from her hands.

When I saw Abaddon's name, address, and phone number I could breath again. I felt the weight of the world was lifted off my shoulders as I stared at the exact thing I had longed for.

"This is it Mikayla. Thank you. Now I have to get you all safe and get out of here." I told her as I gave her a quick hug and my uncle rushed back into the room.

"We gotta go. It's movement outside." Chubb said.

After that we hurried out of the apartment and back to apartment three. Cassie was sitting on the floor in the middle of the other crying girls as we rushed in.

"Come on Cassie we have to go. We'll call the police in the car. You all are safe now and help is on the way." I said as Cassie got up and me, her, and Chubb walked towards the door.

"Wait. Wait. What's your name? You saved our lives." Mikayla asked as I turned back to her and gave her the same name I had given Caroline.

"I'm Quintika and we're the Tortured Souls." I said before we ran from the house and left the girls standing there.

We were over the fence and back at the car in less than a minute. Once we were there we got inside as my uncle threw the bag of evidence in the trunk then he jumped back behind the wheel, and we pulled off. I sat in the passenger seat holding the book feeling better than I had ever felt. I couldn't even talk as I handed Cassie my phone and she called the police. All I could do was picture my reunion with Abaddon. Thoughts of torturing him like I had done Tony danced in my mind the entire drive. I didn't snap out of it until we made it to my uncle's trap and he told us to get out.

"Grab anything you want out of the car cause I'm having my boys get rid of it. I'll get you something else to ride when you're ready to go." he said as me and Cassie quickly grabbed our things then went into the house behind him.

I threw down my bags and plopped down on the couch as my emotional strain set in. I must have been exhausted too because I woke up sometime later to the sound of the news.

"Four missing girls were found today in Harlem in what appears to be a house of torture. One of them was abducted from Los Angeles and then trafficked here to upstate New York. They all were abducted months ago by a man named Tony Moretti. Moretti was found dead at the scene, but there are no viable suspects in his murder." the white female news reporter said before she turned it over to a man in front of the house.

"Well Alice one of the girls rescued said it was three vigilantes that saved them today." the male news reported said before he placed the mic in front of a short white girl. She was one of the girls who Cassie had comforted after the rescue.

"It was this beautiful lady. An angel. She said her name was Quintika. Actually, it was three angels, and they call themselves the Tortured Souls. Thank you all so much. You saved our lives." the girl said as she cried, and the news reporter said they were lucky indeed.

"Police aren't looking for any suspects in the murder of Moretti and we have no leads at this time. All we have is a happy ending for four families who were looking for missing kids. Kudos to the Tortured Souls for giving them those happy endings. We'll bring more information to you as it develops. This is Tim Waller of

ABC7NY singing out." The news reporter said and soon as he was done my uncle turned the TV off.

I stared over at him beside me on the couch before I glanced over at Cassie in the chair.

"I guess we are heroes huh?" I asked as Cassie laughed and my uncle said we were.

Too bad I didn't feel like one though because suddenly my heart was heavy. I remembered how Tony had spoke on my daughter, the dream I had, and how Justin wasn't answering the phone. That's why as my uncle and Cassie smoked and drunk to celebrate, I got up to make a call. I dialed Justin's cell and then our house number as I walked into the kitchen, and I still got no answer. Fed up and worried out of my mind, I dialed Justin's dad Rick's number. Rick answered on the first ring frantic as I heard chatter in his background.

"Hey Rick, this is Jessica. Do you know where Justin and A'Miracle are? I've been calling but I get no answer. My dad is supposed to be there but he's not answering either." I said as I heard Rick gasp then whimper into the phone.

I felt my heart stop beating at that moment as I waited on him to answer my questions. When he did I wish the words had never left his lips.

"Jess. Oh Jessica. I've been trying to contact you. Justin… he's… and Your dad… oh Jessica. Just come home." Rick said as I screamed for him to tell me what had happened.

"What about Justin and my dad? Rick where is A'Miracle? Where is my daughter?" I asked as I cried and walked back into the living room.

My uncle and Cassie could hear what I was saying so they stood by on go.

"A'Mircale is gone Jess. Somebody took her."

That was the last thing I heard before everything suddenly went black.

"This is ABC7, Los Angeles. Welcome to the morning news!"
Boomed in my ears as I tried to lift my heavy head up off the soft
cushion it was on. I opened my eyes slowly as I cautiously lifted my
head and sore body up off the seat. I looked directly into my uncle's
face once I was up, and he smiled as he gripped my hand. He told me
that we had landed in LA and that we would find out what was going
on soon.

"You just relax Jess. I don't need you passing out again." Chubb
said as Cassie chimed in.

She grabbed my left hand from the seat she was sitting in beside
me on the small charterer plane my uncle had gotten us.

"Yeah just stay calm Jess. Everything will be alright." Cassie
said as I stared at her still numb as I heard Rick say that A'Miracle
was gone in my mind.

All I could do was stare as I wondered where she was at and if
she was okay, then the news story caught my attention again.

"Prominent public figure and music mogul Aries Marshall was
found unresponsive in the Brentwood home of his daughter Dr.
Jessica Michaels at around four am on Sunday. The daughter of
famed criminal psychologist Dr. Jessica Michaels and up and coming
architect Justin Michaels was also reported missing from the scene
and Aries was s-…" The reporter said as my heart raced, and tears fell
from my eyes.

I unfastened my seat belt and sat forward in the seat as the TV
snapped off and my uncle suddenly stood up. He had a flushed,
worried expression on his face as he told me everything was okay.

"Jessica just stay calm. Everything will be alright. I spoke with
your mom not long ago and the police are doing their jobs.
Everything will be fine." My uncle Chubb said in a broken, shaky
tone as he choked back tears.

I knew he was lying from the way that he couldn't make eye contact with me and from the aching, dullness which had developed in the pit of my stomach. It was a shallow, bleak, almost catatonic like pain that let me know that the light I once had within me was almost out. Without my family I had nothing to live for. Nothing to hold me back from being a force eviler than Abaddon. I would unleash my wrath on everyone in my way if those I loved we're taken from me. That's all I could think about as the pilot cleared us to leave the plane and I stood on my shaky legs. Chubb grabbed my arm and helped me to the door as his tense shoulders rose and fell. Before we stepped out he stopped and stared down at me as I looked right through him with glossy, emotionless eyes. I didn't know how to feel, and I wasn't sure if I wanted to.

"Jess, say something. Don't do this baby. Please don't go back into a catatonic state like you did after…" my uncle said as I stared at him and heard what he said.

I heard him, but I was in such a state of shock I couldn't process my emotions. It was like the screams in my throat and the pain in my heart was covered by an invisible cap and the pressure within me was building up. I knew it would bust soon and everything I felt would coming pouring out. I just didn't know when it would happen and how. All I did know was that I was devastated, and I knew Abaddon was behind that devastation. I knew I had to get to him too and in order to do that I had to appear sane. I couldn't shut myself off again and go into that dark place. That would get me nowhere but locked up in the very place I had sent patients. That's why I actually looked back at my uncle as he continued to tell me it would be okay.

"Just say something Jess and let me know you're alright." Chubb said as I swallowed the lump in my throat and told him I was good.

"I'm as good as I can be Unc. I just need to know what's going on. I need to find my daughter. Abad-…" I started to say before my uncle cut me off. He glanced around before he began to guide me down the steps.

"Well talk about that later Jess. Let's see what's going on first."
Chubb said but, in my heart, I already knew.

I had been running the streets and wreaking havoc in Abaddon's
world like he couldn't touch mine. I had been so bent on saving
Cassie and finding Mikayla that I left my own princess vulnerable.
A'Miracle getting snatched was all my fault and I would never forgive
myself.

My guilt almost ate me alive as I got into the waiting car my
uncle had arranged and got lost in the emotions surging, suppressed
inside of me. As we rode I glanced out of the window at the beautiful
LA landscape I once admired and all I saw was gloom. My once
happy world was shattered, and the glass house Justin and I had
created was crumbling down all around me. I was a shadow of my
former self as I sat frozen while we pulled up in front of the
emergency room at Kaiser Permanente, Baldwin Hills Hospital. My
uncle helped me out and Cassie opened the door as we walked into
the emergency room. The screams trapped in my heart made me feel
nauseous as my uncle walked me to the front desk.

"Aries Marshall. What room is he in?" my uncle asked as a tall,
white nurse stood up.

She asked him his name and what our relation was to the patient
before my uncle went off.

"I'm his brother bitch and this is his daughter Dr. Jessica
Michaels - and that's his niece. Where the fuck is he? Damn all these
questions." my uncle Chubb said as he banged his massive hand on
the desk irate like I was inside.

He had told me to stay calm because everything would be okay
but from the way he was acting I knew that it wasn't. The nurse
obviously knew that too because as she suddenly stared at me I saw
tears in her eyes.

"Oh Dr. Michaels, I'm so sorry ma'am. Your father's in room 409." the nurse said before she quickly dropped our gaze and my uncle sucked his teeth.

He banged the desk one last time before he turned and led me to the elevators. My heart raced as we stepped inside, and it took us to the fourth floor. Cassie held by hand as my uncle led me out and straight to my father's rom. At the door I got stuck unable to move. I was afraid of what awaited me. I had good reason for such fear too because when the door opened I got a glimpse inside. I saw my father hooked to a ventilator with other tubes running from every inch of his skin. The gentle giant who had protected me all of my life was laying broken with a huge bandage on his head. I felt my knees buckled as my uncle held me up and my mother, Allana, stepped out and wrapped me in her arms. She cried like a baby as she rubbed my back, and I knew that my worst nightmare had come true. She didn't even have to say the words as she told me everything would be alright.

"He's gone Jess. They just have his body holding on. I wouldn't let them pull the plug until you got here." my mother said as I looked into her swollen, tear-streaked face and that cap over my emotions flew off.

I fell into her arms and cried as my uncle wrapped us both in his arms. We all cried for the smooth, kind-hearted gangsta who had turned his dream into a fortune. My daddy started a billion-dollar company from three dollars of drug money and put the whole hood on. He was loved by many and would be missed most by those he loved. My father was the glue that held us altogether and without him I fell apart. I broke from my mama's embrace and ran into the room as the smell of death met me at the door. I knew that dull, stale smell from my many days of living in Abaddon's version of hell. I knew the way it made goosebumps pop up on your arms too as I walked towards the bed and my stomach churned. I cried and shook as I got to the edge of the bed and my father's battered, swollen face came into view. He had a patch over his right eye and there was a long stitched up cut from his bottom lip to the middle of his forehead. My daddy looked like he had gone to war, battling an army alone it was a battle he lost and in that exact moment I lost a part of me too.

"Daddy. Ohhhh daddy. Daddy I'm so sorry. Daddy please. Just wake up." I cried as I held his hand.

My mama walked up behind me and rubbed my back as she cried, and I could feel Chubb and Cassie's hands on each of my arms. They all cried with me and tried to give me strength, but I could channel nothing but pain. I stared at my father's face and memorized each inch as I cried and tried to will him to wake up. Suddenly his heart monitor picked up as he squeezed my hand and I cried out.

"He's squeezing my hand. He's going to wake up." I cried as Chubb ran out of the room to get a doctor.

I kissed my daddy's face and continued to call his name trying to bring him back to me. The heart monitor continued to beep as my daddy's grip on my hand got tighter. I bent down to whisper in his ear as my mama cried.

"I love you Daddy and I'll get him back. I know Abaddon did this to you. I know he has A'Miracle too and I promise I'll get her back. Just wake up daddy. Please." I whispered before I kissed his cheek while a tear fell from his eye.

I stood back up as his grip on my hand loosened and the heart monitor went flat.

"BEEEEP…." It rang in my ears as everything in my world came tumbling down.

I stumbled back into the wall and cried as my mama held me and medical personnel ran in. They ushered me and my mama out of the room and into Chubb's arms as they went to work on my daddy. So many people ran in and out we were able to watch it all from the door. I saw them try to resuscitate my daddy without success before the doctor called his time of death as 5:02 am. I fell into my mama's arms and bawled until I passed out. I woke up in a hospital bed as my mama held my hand and Chubb and Cassie stood by concerned.

"What happened? Where am I? Daddy? Oh my God mama. My daddy gone." I cried as my mama wrapped me in her arms as she gently rubbed my hair and told me.

She sobbed gently, more controlled as she told me everything would be alright.

"Aries is in a better place baby. Daddy is with the father of all father's now. Please Jess. You have to remain calm. They had to give you something after you passed out and became unresponsive. You're stable now baby so just breathe." my mama said as I listened to her and took deep breaths.

I tried to suppress the screams building up in my throat as she looked me in the eyes.

"Mama, what happened? Where is Justin and what happened to A'Miracle?" I asked as my mama wiped away my tears and then sat down next to my bed.

She stared at me with her beautiful, wise eyes as she prepared to give me some of her naked truth. My mama couldn't sugar coat her words even if it was something tragic. She never lied to me in my life so I knew she would tell it all.

"Tell me mama." I said as she gently rubbed my cheek.

"Baby somebody broke into the house. They tried to make it look like a robbery by taking a little cash and some jewelry. However, we believe A'Miracle was the main target because they wouldn't leave without her. Justin and your dad put up a fight while they had A'Miracle hidden in the panic room, but it was too many for them to fight. They shot your dad twice in the head and that's how he ended up here." my mama said as tears ran down her face to match the ones that dripped from my chin.

"What about Justin? What happened to him?" I asked my mama as she suddenly looked away.

"He was stabbed multiple times and shot in the stomach, but his wounds are recovering quickly. It's not the physical aspect that's holding Justin up." my mama said as I reached over and grabbed her chin to turn her face back to me.

"What's wrong with Justin ma?" I asked as panic built up inside me.

I started to get up out of the bed as my mama pushed my legs back down and told me to hold on.

"Hold on Jessica. You have to stay in bed until you're cleared. I'll tell you. Just give me a second." My mama said as she swallowed hard, and I laid back in the bed.

I watched her face as she settled back in the chair, and I already knew what she would say.

"He's just like you were when we brought you back Jess. He just sits there in this daze with his fists clenched. They said he must have seen A'Miracle being taken and what happened to Aries because he completely shut himself off." my mama said as she sniffled, wiped her eye and then stared back at me.

I swallowed the lump in my throat as my body began to shake.

"He needs you Jess. The doctors don't know how to bring him back. But I think I do. I think he just needs you. That's why I need you to stay calm." my mama said as cried and covered my face with my hands.

I knew exactly what was going on and I knew the dark place Justin had gone to. I knew I was the only person who could rescue him from that hurt inside too. That's why I calmed myself and did everything asked of me that day so that I could be discharged. When the doctor said I was clear to go I went straight to the floor Justin was on. My mama, Chubb, and Cassie followed me up and waited outside as I ran in.

"Justin. Justin, I'm here." I said as I cried and ran over to him.

He sat motionless in the bed and stared towards the window as his green eyes flickered with rage. His body was deathly still as his chest rose and fell from the heavy breaths he was taking. I knew that he was there, beyond the darkness and pain, crying a million tears. I knew that I could pull him out of that darkness he was trapped in too as I wrapped my arms around his neck and pressed my forehead to his.

"Justin, I'm here baby. It's me I'm back. I'm here and we're going to get A'Miracle back. Snap out of it, Justin. Baby. Come back to me!" I said as huge tears fell from my eyes and landed on Justin's face.

I kissed his head as I held his hand and stared into his lifeless eyes.

"I'm here Justin. Baby, if you don't wake up we can't find her." I said as I felt his hand move in mine then I leaned down to whisper in his ear. "I know where you are, and I know you feel his presence. He has her. We can get her back though Justin. I already know where he's at. I can't do this alone though baby. I need you. A'Miracle needs you. Please Justin." I cried as I kissed his lips and he kissed me softly back.

I couldn't help but to squealed as I pulled away and looked into his face. Justin was back but he was no longer the soft spoken, loving, logical man I had left. He was the devious, malice, downright evil Justin I had seen on occasion while living in hell. I knew that hateful man oh too well, so I was sure we'd get my baby back. Justin reassured me too as he grabbed me in his arms, and I cried.

"Our baby Justin. He has her. I know it was him. Oh my God. We have to kill him." I sobbed as Justin rubbed my hair and growled softly while my mama, Chubb, and Cassie stood by.

Justin told me that he loved me as he grabbed my face in his hands.

"It was him. I heard his voice right before they shot me. He has our baby and we're going to get her back. I let her down baby. I couldn't protect her. I'll never make that mistake again. I'm going to destroy everything Abaddon loves. I'm going to finally make us whole again." Justin said as he growled and cried as he held on to me.

I stayed in his embrace the rest of the day as Chubb and my aunts helped my mama prepare for my father's funeral. I couldn't do anything but sit there in Justin's arms and wonder about my baby. That's all that remains on my mind the three days that followed as

Justin was held for evaluations and my mama found peace in organizing my father's farewell. I moved through those days like a zombie going from a nearby hotel then straight back to the hospital.

That Saturday, the day of my father's funeral was the most heartbreaking, and sobering day of my life. I hadn't even been able to return to my house let alone truly face the fact that my dad was gone, and my daughter was missing. It became real though as Justin held my arm and ushered me into the huge church. He had just been discharged himself, but he stood tall, and determined as he led me in. The massive building was packed with mourners both regular people and celebrities alike. They all stared up at me with sorrowful eyes as Justin led me down the aisle and to the front of the church behind Chubb and my mama. Cassie sat on the end beside me once we got to the front and the service automatically began.

"Good evening everyone, we're gathered here tonight to honor the life of the great man who was Aries Marshall." the preacher began as I stared straight ahead into my father's face.

He looked so peaceful as he laid in the gold casket with purple lining inside. I smiled to myself as tears rolled down my face and I remembered him planning that part of his funeral.

"When a king like me dies, he has to be buried in gold. Purple lining must touch my skin to represent royalty entering the pearly gates." my daddy had said one night after an album release party as he drunk champagne out of a bottle and all his friends laughed.

They thought he was drunk and just joking but after hearing it throughout my life I knew it was the truth. It was his real wishes and my mama honored everything he said. She had him draped in silk on his bed of purple looking like a real King.

"Aries was a great man who touched many and left this Earth way too soon. He leaves behind many heavy hearts but none as heavy as his wife and daughter." the preacher said as he looked over at us and all eyes in the building swung our way.

I laid my head on Justin's shoulder then overwhelmed as Boyz to Men began to sing.

"Although we've come. To the end of the road. Still I can't let go." The group sang as they walked down the aisle beside me and up to the pew.

They sung from their hearts as I sobbed into Justin's chest once their song was done they talked about how my daddy had impacted their lives. By the time they were done there wasn't a dry eye in the house. I cried and held on to my daddy not wanting to let go at the viewing. Justin had to pull me away as I shook and sobbed. I felt responsible for my father's death, Justin being hurt and A'Miracle being snatched. It was all my fault because I had provoked Abaddon, so it was me who had to finish it. I told Justin that as we stood outside the church after the funeral, and he told me I wouldn't do it alone.

"We're going to get rid of Chubb and send Cassie home then WE'RE going to get our child." Justin said with a bass in his voice that let me know he was serious.

I rambled off the things I had done and my reason for saying I had to go alone.

"I provoked him baby. I brought him out of hiding. I have to end him and get our baby back." I said as Justin grabbed me in his arms and told me we would do it together.

"Were going to find her Jess. We're bringing her home." Justin said as he held me, and I suddenly felt another hand on my back.

"Yes we will find her. You too aren't leaving me out. If you have to go back to hell I'm coming along too." Maria said as my head snapped around and I stared into her beautiful face.

She was all grown up with her deep, loving eyes. I quickly pulled her in to me and Justin as we hugged her, and she said she was with us until the end.

"I've been here since day one when Justin's dad called me. I already know what you're thinking and you both of you are correct. He was here. He has here. We have to get her back." Maria said as we let go of our group embrace just as my mama, Chubb, and Cassie walked out of the church.

We gave each other knowing glances before we pushed our plan to the back of our minds. We went through the motions of the burial before we made an appearance at the reception which was held the Ritz Carlton near the church. I barely ate or even spoke to people as they celebrated my father's life because I was so trapped in my thoughts. I was trapped in my pain of losing the first man I had ever loved. My father was my everything and without him I felt lost. I felt even more astray knowing my daughter was gone. I knew the only thing that would make me feel better was killing Abaddon and getting my baby back. That's why when the night came to an end, I pulled my uncle and Cassie to the side and told them it all was over.

"Unc, thank you for all you have done but you can go home now. Cassie I'm putting you on a plane to Minnesota tonight. I got in contact with your mom, and she'll be waiting on you in the morning. I'm done with revenge and trying to be a fucking superhero too. I'm just done! I'm just going to disappear for a minute and get myself together." I said as my uncle sucked his teeth and glared at me suspiciously.

He knew that I was lying and wouldn't let go so easily but he had no proof. He did have that gut feeling that I was up to something, so he spoke on it after he hugged me.

"I know it's more to that niece but you're hiding it from me. Know that I'm here to help no matter what. Okay?" my uncle asked as I nodded my head at him.

He let me go after that then I grabbed Cassie's hand and we walked outside as Justin followed.

"I had all of your bags put in Justin's car so you're ready to go to the airport." I told Cassie as we walked to the car, and she said that she didn't want to go.

She knew just like my uncle did that our mission was far from over. It was over for them though and I told Cassie that as we got into the car.

"Its best if we part ways now, but you will see me again. We don't need you on this journey though because shit is about to get dark." I told Cassie as I stared at her in the rearview and she nodded her head.

She didn't even argue as Justin pulled out of the parking lot and drove us towards LAX. Cassie said nothing until we got there, and I got out to help with her bags.

"I have to thank you again for everything Jess. I'll never be able to repay you for all you've done for me. I wish you'd let me help but just know I'm only a call away if you need me. You're like the sister I never had. I love you Jess." Cassie said as tears fell from my eyes and I hugged her tightly to me.

I told her that I loved her too and I'd see her again soon before I let her go. After that I watched her pick up her bags and disappear into the airport. I got back into the car with Justin and Maria as tears fell from my eyes.

"Okay baby, it's time to go home before we make our way to hell." Justin said as I nodded, and he drove us towards our house.

When we pulled up and I saw the yellow crime scene tape, my heart fell to my feet. Everything became real again as Justin and I held hands and made our way into the house. Blood and the stifling smell of death hit us as soon as we were in the door. Justin squeezed my hand and told me to be strong as we made our way through the disheveled first floor. Everything we owned was either broken or flipped over. I picked up a picture of me, Justin, and A'Miracle from the summer before as he let my hand go to explore the rest of the room. I stared at our happy faces as tears fell from my eyes and I turned the frame over in my hands. As soon as I did I spotted the pink postcard with butterflies all over it taped to the back.

'Come find us!'

Was written in red ink that appeared to be blood. It was a note from Abaddon letting us know that our worst nightmare had in fact come true. My hands shook as I held the frame in my hand and Justin called my name.

"Jess, what is it?" Justin asked as he walked up beside me and took the frame from me.

He read it as Maria joined us and Justin filled her in.

"It's a note from Abaddon. He has A'Miracle and he's taunting us. He said come and find them." Justin said as he shook in rage while I nodded my head.

I thought about that brown book I had in my possession that would lead us right to him.

"He thinks we don't know where he is but he's sadly mistaken. We're going to take back our baby and end this hell once and for all." I said as I swallowed back my tears and heard my daddy's voice in my mind.

That was all I needed to send me on my quest with a vengeance. It was one thing to torture and hurt me, but it was blood on my baby. I would walk through hell with gasoline thongs on for that little girl. That's exactly what I intended to do too as I left the house enraged.

I stared at Justin as we left the house, and he took on a whole new demeanor. He was no longer that quiet gentle man I had married years ago. I saw hate and fire but in his emerald eyes as he got on his phone and barked orders like the boss he was. It wasn't construction related orders though. No, my man set up chartered planes, cars, and a place for us to stay in Delaware as we walked back to the car. He didn't request, he demanded as he opened the trunk and I stopped to peer inside. It was neat in the back of his brand-new Tahoe as I stared inside and saw nothing was there but freshly shampooed carpet. What I didn't see was just beyond the floorboard that Justin lifted up to reveal an arsenal. I stared at him stunned as he continued to talk on the phone and pull guns out. He pretended not to see my face as Maria walked to the other side of me. I glanced at her still flabbergasted and saw that just like Justin, her face had changed too. Gone was the sweet little innocent church going Maria who cried in my arms many nights while we were living in hell. Her deep, long brown hair still shined in the sunlight but the glow in her big brown eyes had turned dark. Maria stood there looking at Justin intently until he pulled a Scorpion Evo 3 submachine gun from the bag. I knew about that type of heavy artillery from my training to catch Abaddon. What I didn't know was how my architect husband and little religious Maria knew about it. I found out though when Justin suddenly leaned back and placed the massive gun into Maria's waiting hands. She grabbed it like it was a life raft as she sighed and growled lightly. I looked over at Justin confused as he nodded his head and ended his conversation.

"Have the plane ready, the car on standby, and the house stocked with all we need. It's a go. Operation Take down is in full effect. I'll call you with further instructions once we land." Justin said sounding like a fucking Army Sargent as he hung up the phone and stared at me.

I was sure he could see the confusion on my face as he wrapped me in his arms.

"Jess, I know you're confused right now, and you have every reason to be. You know how you told me about all of your secret training with Maria today and how you have been out killing, trying to get to Abaddon?" he asked as I nodded my head and then held my breath.

I had no idea what Justin was about to tell me but as my heart raced and my hands began to shake, I knew it would be something that would change everything.

"Well baby, I wasn't mad about you not telling me because I had a little secret of my own. A few years ago, I joined an elite team of vigilantes and have been searching for Abaddon. I found information this weekend when I was supposed to be on a fishing trip with my boys. I found information that could ensure we get our hands on him. I was coming home to regroup before I made a move, and that's when everything happened. I was taken totally off guard by the attack Jess." Justin said as he lowered his head and his shoulders rose and fell as he took in deep breaths.

I rubbed his back and let him know that no matter what he was going to tell me, I'd still be there. He sensed that too as he slowly looked up and continued.

"That's why I wouldn't let you blame yourself. This is my fault. I led them here unknowingly and now I have to find then and get our baby back. I promise I'll get her back Jess. I'm so sorry baby." Justin said through clenched teeth as I watched a tear fall from his eye.

I wiped it away as I shook my head no and told him it wasn't his fault.

"This is no one's fault but Abaddon's ad he should be the one who should be punished. Not You. We'll make him suffer baby. I got information on him too. I got a book with an address in Delaware." I told Justin as I hugged him then I let him go.

He told me he had tracked them to that same state and asked me what the address was as he ran his fingers through his hair. I quickly reached over the seat and grabbed my bag before I pulled out the brown book Mikayla had given me. I flipped through the pages and then read off the address while Justin growled.

"That's one of the pleasures houses they keep the kids at. That's the address I just secured. I've had my men on it for days now, watching and waiting for Abaddon. He hasn't shown up yet but I'm sure he will." Justin said as I handed him the book and watched Maria quickly load her gun.

"When he does we need to be there." I said as I continued to stare at Maria looking like a Mexican GI Jane.

I could do nothing but smile and nodded my head after she stuck the massive gun down the side of her pants then grabbed a hunting knife from Justin's bag. She was ready for war as she glanced over at me and smirked then said, "Lets go get our baby back."

She didn't have to tell me twice as I grabbed the entire bag from the back and through it on the floor on the passenger side. I jumped in as Justin and Maria did the same and he pulled off.

We all rode in silence to the small private airport a few miles from our home, as thoughts of revenge surged through our minds. I couldn't stop my heart from racing as I worried about my daughter in the grasp of the devil. Although Abaddon's was A'Miracle's biological father he was still the monster who had kidnapped and raped me. He was a menace, a predator, the devil in the flesh. He was also the diabolical entity that held my daughter's life in his hands. I hated to admit it, but Abaddon's had all the winning cards while holding me and Justin's lifeline in his grasp. A'Miracle was our everything and without her we were no good. That's why we were so determined to find our baby and end the nightmare that was Abaddon's. That was apparently on our faces too as we pulled on to the airstrip and got out with tight grimaces on our faces and bags loaded with guns in our hands.

"Well, Mr. Michaels. How are you today sir? Everything is set up just like you ordered. May I take your bags?" A tall, stern looking white man dressed in flight clothes said in a shaky tone as he eyed Justin's expression.

He looked from him, to me, then Maria before he glanced back at Justin again. I could see fear and caution in his eyes as Justin growled out no before he commanded that the man get ready for take off.

"Yes sir. Right away." The man, I found out was the pilot said as he scurried up the stairs.

Justin turned back to look at me and forced a smile before he grabbed my hand and kissed it.

"I'm sorry your going to see me like this again Jess, but through it all know that I love you. Papa's got a brand-new bag now though. It's nothing but heartaches and headaches until we get our baby back." Justin said as pain and anger flickered in his eyes and he gently kissed my lips.

I nodded that I understood before he grabbed my hand and led me up the steps into the plane. Maria got on behind us and once we sat down the pilot closed the door.

"Okay, we are prepared for take off in less than ten minutes. We will arrive in Delaware in a little under five hours. Please fasten your seatbelts and prepare for a smooth ride" the pilot said into the intercom as he stood by the cockpit, and we fastened our seatbelts.

He disappeared behind the door as Justin grabbed my hand and leaned over to kiss my head.

"I love you baby. Now rest until we get there." Justin said.

I nodded as I curled up on his shoulder and closed my eyes while he got on the phone. I listened to Justin's cold, stern voice ramble off orders as I fell into an instant slumber. I dreamed about Justin and I happy again living in bliss with A'Miracle and no sight of Abaddon. That's how I wanted my real life to be, but I knew that wasn't possible. Not even in my dreams. That's why I wasn't surprised when my beautiful dream turned into that reoccurring, blood curdling nightmare that often left me in a cold sweat, reliving my past. I saw A'Miracle trapped in a cage, bloody and being tortured by Abaddon. Her beautiful, dark eyes that were once filled with life were bleak and dismal as she looked my way.

"Mommy help me please. I want to come home. Mommy please save me." A'Miracle cried as I tried to break free from the ropes that held me.

Even in my dream my anger and anxiety consumed me as I screamed out to Abaddon to let her go.

"LEAVE HER AND TAKE ME! TAKE ME YOU EVIL BASTARD!" I yelled as I broke free from my ropes and ran over to him.

I picked up a bat along the way and swung it at his head as soon as I was within arm's reach. I missed him as he jumped back and quickly snatched me up by the neck as he laughed.

"Yes, I will take you my Jess. And I'll take our daughter too. I'll have you both soon. I want your bodies as well as your souls. But for now, I'll take your heart!" Abaddon said as he cackled and each chuckled rippled through my veins like electricity.

I felt enraged and terrified at the same time as I squirmed in his hands and A'Miracle cried.

"Shhh it's okay baby. Mommy loves you. I'll save you." I said unsure myself.

Abaddon showed me just how wrong I was when he plunged a long, hooked knife into my chest and began to dig my heart out. A'Miracle's screams matched mine as blood ran down my chest and I felt the sharp, excruciating pain. I felt the life began to seep from my body too as Abaddon threw me to the floor and marched towards A'Miracle.

"My baby. My special girl. You'll be Abaddon's special girl forever." He said as he held the bloody knife and used his free hand to open A'Miracle's cage.

I held my chest and gasped as my heart hang by a string, yet I was able to pull myself to my feet. I staggered forward as Abaddon yanked our daughter up by her hair and held her thin body up high over his head.

"Join me Jess. Say that you're home to be my first lady. Say it or I will definitely take your heart." Abaddon said through clenched teeth as he glared at me.

His dark, cold, calculating eyes burned right through my skin to my soul and I shivered as his coldness entered me. I cried as I shook my head no and he did the unthinkable.

"Noooo!" I yelled I watched Abaddon swing my baby like a rag doll and bang her body into the floor.

She crumbled like paper beneath his weight as I lunged towards him with the knife he had used to cut me. I intended to drive it right into his black heart, but Abaddon was waiting with a blade of his own. He stuck it deep into my stomach as he whispered in my face with clenched teeth.

"You won't live with me Jess, so I won't let you live without me! Die!" He said in his evil tone as he stabbed me repeatedly.

I could feel the pain and almost feel the warmth of the blood oozing down my stomach as I woke up still in Justin's arms and screamed.

"Jess. Baby its alright. I got you baby. He will never hurt you again and he won't hurt I'll baby. I promise you that." Justin said with conviction as the pilot got on the intercom.

"We are approaching our secured landing strip in Delaware right now." The pilot said as we braced ourselves for the landing.

I held on to Justin's arm as we touched down on the landing strip and flew to a sudden stop. Once the pilot had the aircraft secured we descended the steps and got into the waiting all black Lincoln Town car. I got into the passenger seat as Justin and Maria loaded the bags into the trunk. I sat there in a daze as visions of my nightmare filled my mind. I knew that dream meant that Abaddon wasn't going to rest until he got his hands on me. I wasn't going to rest either, not until I killed him and made sure my family was safe. That's why I fought my fear and anxiety as Justin and Maria jumped into the car and he said we were headed to the house. He looked over at me and saw all that I wouldn't say hidden behind my eyes. Justin leaned over and kissed my lips softly before he kissed my eyelids and wiped my tears away.

"Everything is going to be alright Jess. Just wait and see." Justin said before he crunk up. I told him that I was okay as I stared out of the window at all of the trees and opened fields.

We drove from the private airstrip in Middletown Delaware to a small three-bedroom house Justin had secured us on Morning side Place in North Middletown. When we pulled up in front of the small brick house I glanced around the empty streets. There wasn't another house for a block on each side and all there was were fields of grass and trees. It was beautiful and serene like those cozy neighborhoods in the movies. I got out of the truck and walked up the driveway as I took in a deep breath of fresh air. Middletown was the type of place you could settle down and raise kids in. It appeared nothing happened there as I watched old people sitting on the porch a block away, watching cars roll by. When Justin got up on the porch and opened the door, I stepped into a whole new world. The entire living room was set up with surveillance cameras everywhere. There was a long table in the middle of the living room floor that was covered in guns and ammo. I stepped in with a puzzled look on my face as Justin carried the bags in. he looked at me and was about to explain before a tall, young black boy appeared from the kitchen.

"You're here Mr. Michaels. Good. Let's get to work." He said as he shook Justin's hand and smiled.

I looked from Justin to him before Justin introduced us to Anthony, his partner and fellow vigilante.

"Yes, I've been working with Justin for a few years now and I've heard so many things about you Mrs. Michaels. It's a pleasure to finally put a beautiful face to the name." Anthony said as he shook my hand then turned to Maria.

I watched both of them freeze for a second as their eyes met then Maria giggled and said her name.

"It's nice to meet you as well, beautiful Maria. I'll get more acquainted later. For now, though…" Anthony said after he kissed Maria's hand then turned around to the table by the window covered in computer monitors.

"For now, you can go over this surveillance Mr. Michaels and tell me if anything stands out to you. I haven't' spotted Abaddon as of yet and there has been no spotting of A'Miracle. I watched over three dozen boys and girls ages three to nineteen being taken in chains over the past few days. It seems they're arranging something big too because a young, dark hair man in Jaguar is here every day. He kind of favors a younger version of Abaddon. At least that's what I could tell from the pictures." Anthony said as Justin, Maria, and I followed him over to the table.

He handed Justin the pictures and I saw him tense up before he slowly handed them back to me. I glared down at the handsome, evil face of the younger version of Abaddon. Anthony was right. The man looked just like him.

"Is this his son?" I asked out loud as Justin and Anthony went through surveillance.

Justin shook his head as he turned towards me and said what I already knew.

"I bet he is. You know how this sick bastard makes babies." Justin said as he clenched his teeth and I watched all of the veins pop out of his neck.

I could tell just saying that and reliving the fact that our daughter was Abaddon's was driving Justin crazy as he gritted his teeth and stared at the screen. I rubbed his back before I told him I was going to take a shower. I just needed a few minutes to myself to think with so many emotions raging through me. That's why after he kissed me, I grabbed my bag and wondered through the house looking for the bathroom. Once inside I dropped my bag, locked the door, and sat on the toilet to cry. I turned on the shower water to mask the sound of my tears as I peeled my clothes off.

"It's okay mommy. I'm okay. I'll hold on until you get here. Just hurry mommy." I heard A'Miracle's strained voice say in my mind as I stood up and stepped into the shower.

She encouraged me to be strong as I washed away my tears and every fear I had. By the time I got out of the shower I was that vengeful Jess again. The me that had developed from the pain. I walked out of the bathroom dressed in all black as Maria rushed past me to do the same thing I had done. She told me Justin and Anthony were waiting before I made my way into the living room. As soon as I got inside I saw that Justin had changed as well. He was dressed in black cargo pants, black boots, with a long sleeve black t-shirt. He had multiple guns strapped to his waist along with knifes hanging from a holster. I stood back and watched him as he laid out a plan to Anthony and someone on the phone.

"Okay, once the girls are ready we're hitting that house. The fancy dressed, young Abaddon is there now, and I don't want him to get away. Now the plan is we will all descend on the location and my soldiers will take their positions around the perimeter. We will stake things out until baby Abaddon leaves. Once he does, we'll follow him and get a better location on his leader. I got a feeling he's going to lead us right to Abaddon." Justin said as Anthony agreed. "In the meantime, you all will standby and make sure every child in that house remains there. We don't want them moving them or doing shit. If anyone tries to do that it's a shoot to kill order. Once we get back if all is still quiet, we raid the house and save them all. Is that clear?" Justin asked as the man on the phone said he had it.

After that Justin hung up, he looked directly at me.

"We're all set baby. It's time to go get our princess." Justin said as he handed me my gun with the silencer on it.

I grabbed it as I looked into his eyes and saw nothing but love and strength. There was no fear in him, just like it wasn't any back when we were kids. That's what gave me the push I needed to load up on guns and ammo as we waited on Maria. When she emerged ten minutes later, fully dressed and began to strap up, Justin said it was a go.

"Anthony your mission is to keep your eyes on the woman at all times. Protect them with your life." Justin said in a serious tone as Anthony told him he would.

After that he loaded up and grabbed a back full of ammo and we left the house. The sun was just setting as we jumped into a black van that was parked at the curb. Justin told me he had everything covered as he looked at my confused face in the rearview.

"This is what I do baby. Your man got this. Now get ready." Justin said as Anthony pulled away from the curb and we drove towards Wilmington.

That was where Abaddon had the pleasure house set up. It was the address from the brown book. We pulled up one block away from the huge farm house just after eight that evening. Cars lined the driveway and the street as finely dressed men and women filed into the house. I looked up into the rearview at Justin confused as a woman walked up the driveway with a leash in her hand. I wondered what was going on with Delaware's rich and elite as Anthony suddenly chimed in.

"This is what they call a pick party. They have all of the children in the house and the potential buyers get to come in and try them out. Some do sick sexual shit, and some just make them prove they can cook or clean. Once they have picked they go into the auction room and buy the kids they have chosen." Anthony said nonchalantly, and I felt sick at the stomach.

I had never heard such sick, inhumane shit in my life. Not since I had broken away from Abaddon's hell that is. That's why hearing the kinds of things all those kids had to endure ignited the rage in me. I growled as I pulled out my gun and leaned forward in my seat.

"So, they auction them off like slaves to the highest bidder? This is some sick shit. We have to stop this now Justin. These kids are just like we once were. We can't sit idly by." I said as Justin agreed but told me we had to be patient.

"We're here to save our baby first, Jess. We'll help them too, but I have to get a location on A'Miracle first. Young Abaddon is our link to that, so we have to wait." Justin said still maintaining a little of his logical sensibility and getting me to see the big picture.

I sat back after that and just watched the house as more and more people arrived. We sat there three hours as the visitors arriving dwindled down and I felt young Abaddon wasn't coming. I was just about to tell Justin that too and suggest we go in anyway when his red Jaguar suddenly pulled up. I felt my heart beat in my throat I watched his tall, slender, well dressed body step out of the car and hand his keys to the boy doing the valet. He smiled a huge, evil grin as the woman who looked like him too, met him at the front of the car. After that I felt every muscle in my body twitch as they looped arms and walked to the door. The valet driver called him back just as he touched the knob and alerted him of something he had left in the car. I held my breath as I watched him hurry back and grab a long leash coming from the backseat into his hands. He drug something from the backseat and around to the hood of the car, and when I saw the crying little girl dressed in a pink baby doll gown like the one Abaddon used to dress me up in, I couldn't help but to gasp. I held my mouth as I watched him drag her to the door then grab the waiting dark hair woman. They sauntered into the house with their pet little girl as I pledged to make him pay.

"Sick bastard. Did you see that? He has her on a leash. He has to meet a fate just as bad as Abaddon's" I said as angry tears slid down my cheeks.
Justin told me he would get it too as he groaned and jumped on his phone.

"He's here. Change of plans though. I need you to follow him when he leaves. Anthony said he never stays long so be on standby. Follow him, no matter how far he goes and then send me the location." Justin said before he hung up the phone and turned back to me. "As soon as he leaves we're going in. We're finding our baby today." Justin promised me and when I looked into his eyes I knew he meant every word.

That's why I just nodded my head as I cocked my gun and Justin turned back around. We sat there on edge for an hour before young Abaddon and his dark-haired woman left the house. I watched them pull away through the bushes from the next street as the car Justin had ordered followed. As soon as they were out of sight Justin turned to ask if we were ready. Maria held up her submachine gun and nodded before Justin looked at me and I told him I was on go. I was too because my heart was racing as I stepped out the car and adrenaline surged all through me. Justin grabbed my hand and Anthony grabbed Maria as we made our way through the bushes. As soon as we got on the side of the house I heard Justin's phone vibrate. He pulled it out as we crouched in the bush and told the caller it was a go. He had just put the phone back into his pocket when the sounds of grenades and bullets rang through the air. I glanced towards the house and saw three dozen masked men in all black as the kicked the doors open and stormed in. Justin motioned us forward as Maria and I followed him and Antony to a side door that had been blown open. We stormed in with our guns in hand as women and children screamed while customers tried to run and hide. The team Justin had sent in before us didn't care though as they picked them off one by one. I watched an old white lady drape din fur tumble down some basement steps after a masked man took her head off with a pump.

"Down here Justin. You know this is where they keep the kids." I said as one of Abaddon's men popped up out of nowhere and I blew his entire face off.

He had his gun pointed at the back of Justin's head, so I had no choice but to take him out. I wasn't losing my father, my daughter, and my man in a matter of days. That's why I continued to fire behind me along with Maria as Justin and Anthony led us down the basement steps. When we got to the bottom the smell of piss, feces, blood, and death was so strong I couldn't help but to gag. I fought back the waves of vomit threatening to break free as we went through a door into a huge room. It was lined with beds holding bloody, crying kids. Some of them were strapped to the beds naked, while others sat balled up in fear. One little girl about seventeen was strapped to a sex swing hanging from the celling as an old man stuck massive sized dildos up her anus. Her blood curdling screams filled the air as she begged for mercy and the man moaned. Her fear and pain seemed to be turning him on as he stood there with his pants to his ankles and jerked off. He was so wrapped up in the act he hadn't even heard us rush in. Justin and Anthony had already released a dozen of the kids from their chains, yet he still hadn't turned around. He didn't hear anything until I walked up behind him and growled before I stuck my gun to the back of his head.

"Dirty old bastard. It's a special place for you in hell. Tell Tony and Mark I sent you." I said as he turned around and looked me directly in the eyes.

I could tell that he saw the death and destruction within me long before I pulled the trigger and took his life. The man's wrinkled old body fell at my feet as I let off two more rounds into his head to be sure. Maria shot another guard who bursts through the back door of the basement before she ran over and freed the girl. Within minutes of me killing the old pervert we had freed all of the kids from their chains. Justin ushered all of them up the stairs to the basement as they cried, and I searched their faces. I was looking for my daughter amongst all of the chaos, but no matter where I looked she wasn't there. By the time we made it up stairs and outside of the house, I was frantic as I found Justin.

"A'Miracle wasn't there Justin. She wasn't in this house. Where is my baby?" I cried as Justin held me in his arms.

He told me to calm down and pull myself together as his phone suddenly began to ring.

"Yes? Are you sure? Keep your eyes on her." I heard Justin yell before he hung up the phone and told me we had to go. "Keith got a visual on A'Miracle. She's at the house young Abaddon went to. Let's go." Justin said as we both turned around and looked for Maria and Anthony.

People ran all through the yard, bloody and wounded as sirens got closer. I spotted Maria as she ran from the house with her arm around Anthony. Blood covered the side of his shirt as he limped along side her and spit out blood.

"He's hit. Help him Justin." Maria said as Justin ran over to grab Anthony.

I listened with tears in my eyes as Justin told him he would get him to the hospital and Anthony shook his head no.

"I'm dying bruh. I already know it. Just go Justin. Leave me. Go get your little girl." Anthony said as he pulled away from Justin and Maria then fell to the ground.

His body began to shake as soon as he hit the concrete and his eyes rolled into the back of his head.

"Noooo. Oh my God, Anthony no. We didn't even get a chance to get to know each other!" Maria yelled as she bent down and kissed Anthony's lips just as his body grew still.

He was gone and we all knew it as Maria cried and Justin pulled her away. He drug her to the van and then helped her in before we got in and he pulled off. We sped out of Middletown headed towards Wilmington as Justin read off the address.

"That's where our baby is Jess. We're on our way." Justin said as he punched the van we were in to the floor.

We drove past the entire Middletown police force as we made our way out of town and towards the lion's den our baby was trapped in. When we pulled into the affluent neighborhood and found the big white mansion from the address, Justin quickly parked three houses away. It was late, so it was dark all down the street and we were able to stealth up to the house without being noticed. As soon as we got close I saw the red Jaguar young Abaddon was driving parked in the driveway and I knew we were in the right place. I eyed Justin before he nodded, and we followed him to the side of the house. I put my back on the bricks and listened hard as soft cries and classical music filled my ears.

"That's A'Miracle." I told Justin as he nodded then held up his hand.

I watched him as he peered around the corner into the window and froze. I knew then what he saw but I had to see it for myself. That's why I quickly stepped around and peeked over his shoulder to peer in the window. Just inside, there was my baby dressed in a pink tutu standing at a ballet bar as she cried. Her feet bled all over the hardwood floor as the dark-haired woman I had seen with young Abaddon yelled for her to dance harder.

"Get it right or you won't eat today. Or maybe I'll beat you again. Or how about we send you to the brothel with the rest of the unwanted kids!" She yelled at my baby before she sliced her down the back with a whip.

A'Miracle screamed and cried out for me as I shook in rage.

"I don't know why daddy loves you so much. Its clear you're his favorite though. And its for that very reason that I hate you! A'Miracle my ass. How about A' Disaster. Dance bitch!" The girl yelled before she hit my baby again.

I had seen enough at that point. I couldn't even stop my body from shaking I was so mad. I turned around with my gun cocked ready to go to war when something hard hit me in the face. I felt dizzy and unstable as I stumbled back and fired, hitting the man who had hit me. I heard Maria and Justin firing too as masked men suddenly surrounded us. Justin shot two of them in the face and had grabbed one in the sleeper hold when a loud, calculating voice suddenly paralyzed me with fear.

"My Jess is back home with her Knight and Shining Armor and side kick too. I knew you would come home Jessica. I knew you would come back to me." Abaddon said from behind me as I felt the hair on the back of my neck stand up.

I felt flustered and overcome with fear and rage as I held my gun and swooped around. I let of shot after shot into the direction of his voice as he laughed then I felt a blow to my head again. That blow was much harder, and it broke me down to my knees.

"Still resistant huh? I guess I have to train you all over again." Adaddon said as he laughed and walked over to me.

Someone held me up by my hair as I glanced around and saw Justin unconscious on the ground. Blood trickled down his face as I cried and looked in the opposite direction for Maria. As soon as I did, I met her terrified, yet angry eyes just as another guard knocked her out.

"Haha." Abaddon laughed out loud as Maria's body fell and he bent down in my face. "I don't know why you insist on learning things the hard way Jess, but I'm here to teach you. Welcome back home baby." Abaddon said before I spit in his face and told him to go to hell.

He laughed as he stood back up and wiped the spit off his skin with the back of his hand. I watched as his smiling face turned to that distorted, evil mug I only saw in my dreams.

"Have it your way then. Lights out Jess." Abaddon said in a menacing tone before he kicked me right in the face.

I tried to fight the darkness that overcame me after that but as Abaddon's men beat me, I couldn't help but to fade away. All I could do was try to ball up and protect my body as Abaddon's laughter rang in my ears and darkness closed in on all sides of me.

The sound of a child moaning and a low creaking noise awoke me from the nightmare I was trapped in. I tried to open my swollen, blood coated eyes as I lifted my head off the metal I was leaning against. I got my left eye to open enough to look down and see that I was stuffed inside an oversized bird cage high above the ground. Underneath it was exposed electrical wires sitting on a board over top of a filled kiddie pool. It was a booby trap sure to kill me if I was able to get my body erect enough to escape the cage. There was no use in me even thinking about that obstacle though because I was so sore and crouched I couldn't move. All I could do was moan and look around the stuffy, stank, dark room I was in. I could make out Maria over to my left tied to a chair with a metal mask around her face. Blood dripped down her chest to her legs from the various gashes all over her body. She sat there so still and quiet I thought she was dead until I called her name.

"Maria are you okay? Where are we and where's Justin?" I whispered as I cried and turned back to watch the door.

I could hear footsteps in the hall and see the shadows under the door as Justin's groans suddenly filled my ears.

"I think he has us downstairs where he tortures people once again. They're beating Justin in the room next to us. They'll be back for us soon. We have to get out of here Jess." Maria cried as I told her to stay calm.

I said it, but I knew it was easier said than done considering the predicament we were in. No one could be calm in the face of the evil we were up against, not even the most cold-hearted man. I knew that because fear surged all through me as I heard a key go into the door. I crouched down lower in my cage and tried to disappear as someone walked into the room. I didn't even want to look up and see who it was as Justin's groans and cries caused me to shiver. I didn't have to see to know who it was when the hair on the back of my neck stood up. I felt my flesh crawl and a dull lump develop in the pit of my stomach as Abaddon laughed to announce his entrance. He made me feel like weak, trapped, teenage Jess again as I hid my swollen eyes with my hands. I didn't want to see him or look at the smug expression I was sure he had. I found out that I had no choice in the matter though when he stuck a cattle prong through the bars of my cage and shocked me. My leg was pressed up against the rusty metal cage when he touched my arm with the cattle prong, so I got a double dose of jolts. I shook and cried in the cage as foam ran from my mouth and Abaddon circled the cage and laughed.

"My tough little Jess. Still the rebel I see. You still don't get the fact that I run this, and you belong to me. I bet this helps drive it in though." Abaddon said as he laughed, and I heard the click of his Italian leather shoes on the cement floor as he walked away.

Once I was sure he was gone, I released the breath I was holding and gasped for air as I looked at Maria then glanced towards the door. I felt both terrified and enraged as I pulled on the cage door trying to break it open. I didn't care about the wires or the possibility of being shocked again, I just wanted to be free. I desired that freedom even more when Abaddon suddenly walked back through the door smiling as he drug A'Miracle behind him on a leash. He had her crawling on all fours like a dog, just like he had done Quintika. She looked drugged out like Quintika did too as she crawled inside the room and stopped at his feet.

"Let her go you sick bastard. It's me that you want. Let them go and I'll stay here with you and do whatever you want. Just let my baby go muthafucka!" I yelled as tears ran from my one good eye like Miss Sophia on The Color Purple.

I felt like her too as I rocked back and forth on my knees while angry tears dripped from my chin. I stared at my baby as she glared back at me like she didn't recognize my face. She had this spaced out, lost gleam in her eyes as she moaned while Abaddon rubbed her hair.

"My Jess and my A'Miracle. My favorite girls are finally home to stay. Does this show you my power and what I'm capable of doing when you don't obey?" Abaddon growled as his voice boomed in my ears like he was on a loudspeaker.

He made me shiver in fear for my baby and growl in rage as I stared out of the cage at him.

"This can all end Jess. It depends on you. I'll give you time to think about it while I go play with daddy's girl." Abaddon's as A'Miracle began to whimper while he pulled her by the leash on her neck.

I cried out that I was ready, so he would let her go, but my pleas fell on death ears. Abaddon slammed the heavy metal door in my face and left me in the birdcage to cry. I cried from my soul for my baby as I heard her cries slowly fade away. My whole mission in life had been to protect her from the hell I lived through and in the end, I delivered her to the devil. Guilt and anger overtook me as I grabbed the bars of the cage and shook them. I tried to rip the rusty metal apart as I screamed like a lunatic.

"Let her goooooo. Please. This is all my fault. Take me. Please let her go!" I cried as Maria tried to soothe me and tell me everything would be okay.

I wanted to believe her but the pain in my heart said something different. That pain told me that just beyond the stairs over my head, my baby was being broken beyond repair. Just the thought caused me to panic as I began to hyperventilate. I grabbed my throat and tried to take in breaths as my lungs felt like they were being squeezed. Everything started to get blurry as I looked around frantically and gasped for air. I felt like I was twelve again and on stage for my last dance recital. I had panicked that day too before my daddy stepped in. He came to the curtain and talked me through it with his smooth, calm voice. I overcame all of my fears as my daddy told me I was brave, smart, and could overcome anything. He gave me strength that I didn't know I had. That was strength I needed right then. Like the true light in my life my father came through at that moment too. He gave me strength from the grave as I heard his voice in my ears.

"You're brave, you're smart, you can overcome anything Lady Bug. Just close your eyes and concentrate on your breathing." my daddy's voice rang in my ears as I did just that.

I squeezed my eyelids closed tightly as I concentrated on my contracted lungs and willed them to inflate. I shook for a minute as I held the bars with my eyes closed, then I caught my breath. I took in deep breaths of air as my daddy's voice slowly faded away. His voice was suddenly replaced by Quintika's as I shook off my fear.

"Jess pull yourself up. You know what you have to do. Remember what you said? Sometimes you have to caress the snake before you chop off his fucking head! Go back to that dark place Jess and get out of there. Play Abaddon like the weak, broken little boy he really is. Get the fuck up Jess. Do this for me. Do this for all of us who suffered at his hands. I love you sis and this not your fault. It is your time to fix it though. You got this Jess!" Quintika's voice said in my mind as I felt jolts of rage shot all through me.

I knew that she was right. I knew what I had to do. That's why when I raised my head and glanced over at Maria, she gasped before she spoke.

"Jess, are you okay? You look different. Everything will be okay. We're going to get out of here." Maria said as I nodded my head at her and told her that she was right.

"We definitely will. You just follow my lead and be ready for the worst." I told her in the calm, cold tone that I almost didn't recognize.

I guess Maria didn't recognize it either because she asked me again if I was okay.

"Yes Maria, I'm okay. Better than I've been for days. Too bad Abaddon won't be able to say the same soon." I said as Maria nodded, and I closed my eyes to think.

I remembered every moment I had spent with Abaddon as well as all of his weakness as I rocked back and forth in that swing. I remained there in that crouched position for days, forced to piss and shit all over myself as I raged. It was the most humiliating thing I had experienced since I had left hell nine years before.

By the time a tall, dark Russian man burst into the room followed by a nurse one day, I was dehydrated and criminally insane. I felt like the animals I studied as my cage was lowered and I growled at the man. He punched me in the face through the bars and told me to shut up before I spit blood in his face.

"Fuck you. Let me go. I need to speak to Abaddon." I said as the guard opened the cage door and yanked me out by my hair.

My legs felt like Jello as he tried to drag me to my feet. It was no use because I couldn't stand on my own, all I could do was curse.

"Let me the fuck go. Take me to Abaddon. Where's my daughter? Where's Justin?" I asked as the guard ignored my questions and handed me over to the nurse.

I glared at his back as he walked over to Maria and the short, stalky nurse held me up. I felt more tears well up in my eyes when I saw the state she was in. Maria was unconscious in the chair as the guard untied her and snatched her up like a rag doll. I cried out her name as he held her in his arms and I watched her take quick, swallow breaths.

"It's okay Maria. I'll get you out of here." I told her as the guard laughed before he left the room with Maria in his arms. "Wait a minute. Where the fuck is you taking her? MARIA!" I yelled as I tried to break away from the nurse, but my legs gave out on me.

I fell face first on the cement floor and almost passed out. I saw tiny birds flying around my head like the cartoons as I pulled my upper torso up from the floor.

"I agree. You do have to learn the hard way ALL THE TIME." the nurse said, and I suddenly caught her voice.

I looked up to see the same evil, red headed Russian nurse who had tortured me the first time I was in hell. I glared up at her overweight Lucy looking ass while she smiled down at me with hate in her eyes.

"His name isn't Abaddon by the way smart, little, rich girl Jessica Marshall- Micheals. His name is Adrik and he doesn't want to see you yet. Now pull yourself together and get the fuck up off the floor before I call Demetri back in here to help you." the nurse said before she grabbed me by my hair and yanked me up.

I felt a little stronger because of the hate pulsating inside of me so I got up on my shaky legs. I knocked her hand out of my hair as she gasped, and I stood back ready to fight. I wasn't afraid anymore and I didn't intend on letting her treat me like a prisoner again. Abaddon had said I was going to be the first lady and that's the only role I was willing to play.

"Don't grab my fucking hair. I know how to walk. I'm not a slave or a kid anymore. I'm the First Lady. Just go ask Adrik." I said as I glared at the nurse with a smug expression while feeling like I would hurl on the inside.

The last thing I wanted to do was be close to or pretend to love someone like Abaddon. I knew that was what I had to do though so I swallowed back my true feelings and waited for my chance. I played that shit good too as I glared at the nurse with one of those evil, Abaddon smiles. My glare was so forceful the nurse knew I would put up a fight. She was much older than before, about 60, so she knew she couldn't take my hands. That's why she did nothing as I stood in front of her and stared her down. Nothing but nod and walk away. I followed her out of the door as the guard she called Demetri reappeared. He walked towards us with an amused look on his face as he nodded at the nurse then glared at me. That didn't scare me, so I asked him where Maria was as he walked behind. Just like I thought, he was weak ass man that couldn't take a woman who stood up for herself. That's why he sucked his teeth and laughed then hit me in the back of the head with his fist.

"Shut the fuck up. You don't ask the muthafucking questions around here. Do as you're told." he said as I laughed, and I walked behind the nurse.

I laughed because I knew exactly what I'd do to him when the time came. He would meet a fate worse than Tony's and that was something I could guarantee. The thoughts of torturing him helped me get through what they had planned next. I held my breath and fought back the screams inside me as I was led deeper, down into the basement. When we arrived at another nasty bathroom like the one from hell, I shook my head and refused to go in. The floor was covered in dirt, blood and bodily fluids just like the walls. The three stalls at the back of the room where black from so much accumulated dirt. There were four rusty shower heads handing from the ceiling on the right side of the room that dripped, brown stagnant water.

"Hell no. Go get Abaddon. I'm not getting in this shit. I know he didn't approve this." I said to the nurse.

Demetrie pushed me in the back further into the bathroom as the nurse shook her head.

"Until he tells me otherwise, you will be treated like everyone else." she said as I watched her walk to the next room and come back holding a cattle prong. "Strip and get in there!" she yelled before she touched me on the shoulder with the rod.

I shook a little as I stood there grounded and growled while the electricity ran through me. I fought the pain and kept my angry eyes planted on them the whole time. I wouldn't give them the satisfaction of seeing me cry even though that shit hurt like hell. I didn't want to be shocked again either, so I shed my clothes as I groaned. I vowed to kill them both in my mind once I was undressed and they both gawked at me.

"Dike ass Wendy's mascot. You're going first." I said to myself as I turned and cut on the shower and let the pissy water wash the blood from my skin.

That shower was everything but refreshing, because I got out smelling worse than I went in. The nurse gave me an old white gown like the one Abaddon would make me wear as a girl and I quickly slipped it over my naked body. I glared at her once I was dressed and she smiled as she grabbed a Scold's Bridle from Demetrie just like the one Abaddon used on Quintika.

"NO. Hell no!" I said as I backed up and Demetrie put me in a headlock.

He held me firmly in his arms as the nurse put the cage over my head.

"Both of you will pay for this. That's my word." I said through clenched teeth before she stuck the spiked mouthpiece of the mask into my mouth.

The razor-sharp spikes pierced my tongue every time I raised it to speak. Blood quickly pooled in my mouth as Demetrie drug me from the bathroom. He led me through the basement past several rooms as I peered inside. I saw Maria in a makeshift infirmary hooked to machines and Justin tied to a wall with a hook in his back. I wanted to cry when our eyes met but the spikes in my mouth prevented that. Instead I just told him to hold on using my eyes and he nodded his head before I was drug away. I fumed as the guard pulled me deeper through the dungeon and up some steps as the nurse talked on her phone behind us.

"She's ready and we're on our way up." the nurse said once we made it to the main floor.

Inside the real house it was beautiful and smelled like apple pie. I glanced around as I counted my steps and made a mental note of how to get back to Justin and Maria. I stared at all of the pictures on the wall as I was led up another stairwell to the second floor. That same old Russian chick Abaddon had pictures of on his wall at the old house, stared back at me. There were family pictures too with him standing in the middle of an army of kids. They were all different races and ages, but they shared his same dark eyes. I shivered as I realized those were all of the rape kids he had. My baby was one of those kids too, destined to live in a family of madness. Not if I had anything to do with it though. I was fighting that fate until my last breath. That's why I remained strong and stood tall as I was drug into a bedroom. I knew it was Abaddon's when I walked in and saw the huge picture of the Russian ballerina over his bed. A huge under the cage like the one from my nightmare was in the middle of the floor. I shook a little as Demetrie drug me closer to it and told me to look at my new home.

"Yeah, you better get used to it because daddy said you will be on punishment for a while." a voice said from behind me as I swung around with the cage on my head and glare at the dark-haired girl as she stood next to the young Abaddon.

I recognized them both from the family picture I had just seen so I knew they were his kids. I guess the girl could see me figuring it out in my mind as she smiled and stepped closer to me.

"Yes, Mrs. Jess, I am Adrik's daughter Amelia. That's my brother Adrian." she said as the boy who looked to be about 24 stepped up and bowed at me before he laughed.

"And I'm Arman; and we're our daddy's favorites." Another boy about 13 said as he stepped into the room.

Unlike Amelia and Adrian who were half Latino and Russian, Arman was mixed with black like A'Miracle. He had thick, curly hair, dark skin and those deep, dark penetrating eyes like his daddy. I learned he had the same evil smile too as he strolled in glaring at me.

"At least we were the favorite until little Miss Ballerina came along. Now we have to share the spotlight with her - and you too." Amelia said as she lit a cigarette then blew the smoke out in my direction.

"What makes you so special Miss Jess? Why are you still alive but or mothers aren't?" she asked as she walked closer to me and motioned for Demetrie to let me go.

He did it and then stepped back as she walked into my face.

"Is it because you're some fancy ballerina? Or because you were a nasty little girl who turned him out? My daddy was always particular to dark meat anyway." she said as she laughed then looked back at her brothers.

They laughed too as I glared at them all while my heart raced in my chest. It took everything in me not to reach out and grab the little, nineteen-year-old psycho chick up by her neck, but I knew it wasn't the time. That's why I just stood there and stared as she turned back around with a sinister look on her face.

"I hate dark meat though…" she said as Arman shouted, "Hey!".

"Well usually anyway. Your daughter and you aren't the exceptions." she said as she hit her cigarette again.

"I'm going to make you lives hell no matter what my daddy says." Amelia said as she blew the smoke in my face then suddenly stuck the lit but into my cheek.

The pain was so searing I couldn't help but to yelp and react. Blood ran from the corners of my mouth as I unleashed a hail of punches on the unexpecting girl. She backed up flapping her arms around wildly like she had ran through a cloud of gnats. That didn't stop my attack though as I delivered a series of forearm strikes and punches into her face.

"Little evil bitch!" I yelled as I grabbed her hair and yanked her to the ground.

I was about to head but her with the cage as Demtrie hit me from behind. He caused me to fly over Amelia's body and bang into the wall. As soon as I was down they were on me as they stomped and kicked me to sleep. I woke up some time later, trapped in that cage under Abaddon's bed. It was dark and stifling under there like I was in a grave. I reached up and felt my face to see the cage was gone and I began to scream.

"What the fuck? Let me out. Abaddon!" I yelled as my tongue throbbed and my dry throat cracked.

I yelled for what felt like hours, but no one was around to hear. No one came for me for days and by the time they did I was soiled again and out of my mind with hunger.

"Please. Please give me water and food. I told Abaddon I'd be a good girl." I gasped as Demetrie pulled me from the box and laughed at my despair.

He laughed at me and told me what a weak bitch I was before he called A'Miracle's name.

"Look at your superhero mommy A'Miracle. She doesn't look so tough no does she? I told you she wasn't coming to save you. She can't even save herself." Demetrie said as I glanced over to the side and noticed my baby standing by the door.

She was all clean and beautiful in her bright yellow dress with her hair pulled up into a curly bun. She looked at me with sorrowful eyes as a tear ran down her cheek.

"Don't cry for her, she's not your mommy anymore. You belong to Adrik. You're apart of a bigger plan. Forget all ties to the life you lived before because you will never return to it again. Now, you stop looking at her and get in there." Demetrie said as he pushed me towards the bathroom door.

I continued to look at my baby and talk to her with my eyes, reassuring her everything would be okay. I heard her cry and run away once I was inside, and I pushed back my emotions. I showered in silence as rage flowed all through me. Once I got out and Demtrie gave me a long red gown to put on, I knew it was time for my act. Abaddon was coming, and I had to gain his trust so he would lower his guard. That's all I thought about as I was led back into the bedroom and Demetrie locked a long chain attached to the wall around my waist.

"Now sit here and be quiet until you're told to speak." Demtrie said as he pushed me on to the bed and then disappeared out the door.

As soon as he was gone I ran over to the picture on the wall and lifted it up. I knew where Abaddon kept his hiding places and when I saw the huge safe behind the picture I smiled. I could feel there were guns inside and that would be my way out. That's why I just put the picture back and sat back on the bed as I thought about the possible combinations to the safe. I had settled on A'Miracle's birthdate at the four-digit code by the time the door swung open. My heart raced in my chest as Abaddon walked in smooth, handsome and as evil as ever with a Hugo boss suit on and evil smile planted across his face.

"My Jess, I heard you were ready to take your place." he said as he walked in and closed the door behind him.

I kept a brave face as my heart beat a mile a minute in my chest. I nodded my head as he smiled and walked closer to me.

"Let's see how ready you really are." he said as he grabbed my hand and pulled me up from the bed.

As soon as I was on my feet, Abaddon wrapped his arms around me as he laughed. He twirled me around the room as he hummed and smelled my hair.

"I've dreamed about this for years Jess. The day you would come back to me. All I ever think about is you and our daughter. June 30th was the happiest day of my life. You made me miss that though, and for that I can never forgive you." he said in a suddenly angry tone as he stopped dancing and threw me to the bed.

I fell back on my back as he straddled my body and glared into my face. His eyes pierced my soul as he stared right through me.

"You can make it up to me though. If you promise to be a good girl." Abaddon said as he sniffed down my neck and I fought back my rage.

I thought about everything I could to take me out of that moment and what he was doing to me. I made a mental note that the code to the safe was my baby's birthday as Abaddon kissed my breasts then ripped the gown from my body.

"You better no resist then if you're ready. I better know you WANT TO be here." he said before he started to take off his clothes then he laid his naked body on top of me.

I closed my eyes and envisioned Justin as I put on an Oscar worthy performance. I did my best to pretend I enjoyed sex with Abaddon as my stomach churned and my flesh crawled. I did a good job too until Abaddon decided to sodomize me. I could do nothing but cry and growl as I held on to the bed and wished it all was over. When it was Abaddon fell down in the bed and wrapped me in his arms. He held on to me like I was his girlfriend and we had just made love. Not like I was a fucking prisoner who had been raped. That was his worse mistake though because before long he had fallen asleep. I glared up into his face and saw the long slash on his cheek I had seen in my dream.

"Muthafucka." I whispered as I slid from under him and to the side of the bed.

I looked back to see he was still asleep before I stood up. As soon as I was up I ran over to the table by the door and grabbed the letter opener I had seen. I grabbed it up in my hand and crept back over to the bed as Abaddon slept peaceful. As I stood there glaring down at him he flipped over to his back, and I watched his neck as he swallowed. His Adam's apple seemed to taunt me as I raised the letter opener up. I was just about to come down with it in his throat when his eyes suddenly popped open. I swung and nipped his neck just as he kicked me. I soared across the room like a sheet of paper in the wind as Abaddon growled.

"Ungrateful, sneaky bitch. Get over here." he said as I tried to crawl towards the door, but he grabbed me in the back of the hair.

"See what you do when I try to be nice? Rotten bitch, now all of you will die here." Abaddon said as he chopped me across the throat and dragged me back towards the box.

I clawed at the ground and tried to fight him off, but I was too weak to do anything. All I could do was moan as he threw me back into the box.

"This is where you will die Jessica and its all your fault."
Abaddon said before he locked the box and slid me back into
darkness which I was sure would be my grave.

To Be Continued….

I remained in that box for weeks laying in my own waste with nothing to eat but crackers and bread. I only got water when A'Miracle would sneak it to me in capfuls from the bathroom faucet. I felt like I was falling apart as I laid there being tortured and raped periodically not knowing what was going on. That's why I was always happy when A'Miracle was able to sneak away to talk and sing to me. That day was no different as my heart raced when I heard her open the door. I waited until I heard the door close, and I was sure it was her before I called out her name.

"Yes, it me mommy. I'm here and I'm going to help you." A'Miracle said before she pulled my box out and I stared up into the light.

It hurt my eyes so bad I had to cover them with my bloody, soiled hands as I told A'Miracle to put me back. She had never pulled my box all the way out when she came, and I was afraid of her being caught. My baby wasn't scared though as she pulled a key from the pocket in her shirt and told me it would be alright.

"They're all gone so we have time to get you all out of here mommy. I just saw daddy, he's downstairs with Maria. They planned on selling them tonight, but we can't let that happen. We have to go mommy." A'Miracle said as she opened my cage and I popped up like a jack in the box.

I hugged her close to me as tears ran down my face and I told her it would be okay.

"I'm so sorry mommy. I never wanted to help them, but they made me. They said I'm one of them and this is the family way. I'm a Michaels Mommy, and you and daddy are my family. I just want to go home." A'Miracle cried as I held her.

I kissed away her tears before I climbed out of the box and sat on the bed to regain my balance.

"You are a Michaels baby, and I'm about to take you home." I told my daughter before I kissed her forehead and then jumped up.

My legs were wobbly from being trapped in that box for weeks, but I didn't care about that. I quickly climbed on the bed and removed the picture to reveal the safe. I punched in the code and just like I thought, 0630 opened it right up. When I peered in at the mountains of cash, diamonds, books, and guns I almost cried.

"We're definitely getting out of here baby. Find me some clothes, shoes, and a bag to put this stuff in." I said to A'Miracle as she scurried off to the closet.

She was back in seconds with a huge duffle bag, some shoes, and a jogging suit that I slipped on before I went to work. I put all of the money, jewels, books, and guns into the bag before I jumped down, put on the too big shoes, and grabbed A'Miracle's hand.

"When we get out of this room you stay close to me." I whispered to her at the door after I set the bag down and pulled out an Uzi out before I cocked it and grabbed her hand again.

I asked her if she was ready as I threw the bag over my shoulder and she nodded her head. I saw fire in her eyes as she smiled at me and said she loved me. I told her I loved her too before I kissed her forehead and got ready. After that she opened the door and we emerged into the quiet hallway. I led my baby down the corridor and then down the steps as my heart beat in my chest. We made it all the way to the front door before I heard voices outside.

"Shh. Wait." I told A'Miracle as I peered out the window next to the door.

I saw Amelia, Adrain, and Arman as they piled out of the car with Abaddon. I quickly pushed A'Miracle back and drug her back through the hall as I asked her if there was another way out. I could hear guards as they walked over head and I stopped to listen. Once they passed over the back hallway we were in I looked at A'Miracle for her response.

"I can get out through the small window in the basement Mommy. That's how I get out to play near the pond. It's a tree house by the lake I read books at." A'Miracle said.

"Okay baby, I need you to get out and go hide in that tree house. Stay there until either me, your daddy or Maria comes to get you. If you see anyone else coming you run and don't stop until you get to help." I told her out of breath as we walked to the basement door.

A'Miracle sucked back her tears and told me she would as I opened the basement door. We had just stepped inside and was about to close the door when the front door burst open. I could hear Amelia singing and Abaddon's laughter as I pushed my baby down the steps. As soon as we were at the bottom I pushed her towards the window and told her to go. Like a little soldier A'Miracle sprinted off as I backed into the wall and surveyed my surroundings. I could hear guards all down the hall, so I put the Uzi back in my bag. I didn't want to alert the psycho family upstairs too soon before I got Justin and Maria out. That's why I found a gun with a silencer on it and cocked it before I crept down the hall. A'Miracle had just closed the window and it clapped shut when one of the guards heard the noise. He came running around the corner towards me blindly and ran right into a bullet. I took his face off as I made my way down the hall to the room A'Miracle said Justin and Maria were in. Another guard upped his gun as I walked towards the door, and I blew his chest out as I kept going. I rushed into the room just as a guard prepared to rape Maria. He had her little legs spread open as he wedged himself between them and Justin yelled. He stopped as soon as he saw me and so did the guard as he turned around. I hit him hard in the face with my gun and he crumbled to the floor as I helped Maria up.

"This you kill." I told her as I handed her the gun and ran over to Justin.

I quickly untied the ropes that held his arms before he grabbed me up and hugged me.

"Baby, you're okay? They told me you were dead." Justin said with tears and vengeance all in his eyes.

"Never baby. You can't get rid of me that easy. These muthafuckas will be dead soon though." I said as I let go of Justin's embrace and thrust the heavy bag on my shoulder in his hands.

He quickly went in it and grabbed out a Glock 17 for each hand and then glanced over at Maria. I looked over at her too as she stuck the barrel of the gun in the gaur's mouth. She pulled the trigger and blew the back of his head out just as a siren went off in the house. The noise was so loud I covered my hands with my ears as I looked at Justin.

"We gotta move now!" he said as he gave me back the Uzi I had and threw the bag over his shoulder. "Stay behind me." Justin said as he led the way out the room and right into waiting guards.

My baby didn't care though, he was on some Rambo, taken shit. I fired off shots behind Justin as he walked calmly down the hall with bullets flying all around his head. He let off precise shots dropping each target as he made his way back to the steps. By the time we made it there a line of dead men laid behind us. That was nothing compared to the bloodbath we made once we were upstairs. As soon as we emerged from the basement door shots rang out and Justin took a bullet to the shoulder shielding me. It didn't slow him down though as we hid behind the door, and he pulled out an AR-15.

"Be ready to run for the door." Justin said before he stepped around the corner and let that bitch rip.

He cut down six or seven men in seconds as me and Maria ran behind him shooting. When we made it to the front door I pulled on the door to see that it was locked.

"To the back!" I yelled to Justin as he tried to kick down the door.

I knew that wouldn't work so I ran down the hall the basement was on as they followed, and bullets flew past our heads from upstairs. When I got to the back hall right before the basement I stopped as I heard someone sniffle. I held up my hand telling Justin and Maria to stop as I walked to the closet door. Justin stood at the end of the hall and fired upstairs as I snatched the door open. When I did, I stared down at Amelia and Arman crouched together as she pointed a gun at me.

"Just leave us alone and you will live." she said as I glared at her.

I could see Maria from the corner of my eye as she got into position, so I raised my gun. Ameila smiled like she had won as she squeezed on the trigger then a shot rang out. Maria put a bullet right through her forehead that sent brains flying all over Arman and the wall. He screamed like a little girl as he shook beside his sister's dead body and begged for his life.

"I'm just a kid. They made me do all of this. Please let me go." he pleaded as a part of me, the mother in me, wanted to show mercy.

However, the smarter part of me knew that he was just like his daddy. That's why I smiled as I lowered my gun and asked him how we could get out.

"In the back is the sunroom, go into the closet. It's a door to the outside that's always unlocked because that's where Amelia goes to smoke. At least she used to. Please let me go." Arman said as he cried and glanced over at his sister.

"Thanks for that information but I can't let you go. You're just like him. A menace a plague and you have to die." I said.

"So is your daughter. She's one of us too bitch." Arman said as his face turned all evil and distorted just like Abaddon's.

"She's nothing like you." I told the boy before I shot him twice in the head.

I left his little body limp on the floor as I told Justin to come on.

"The sunroom!" I yelled as I turned ready to break for it.

I didn't get a chance too though before Abaddon's laughter filled my ears and he let off a single shot. He hit me in the side as I spun around, and Justin charged at him firing shots. I fell to my knees holding my side as Maria ran to my aid and I watched six bullets fly into Abaddon's chest. He fell to the floor at the end of the hall as I gasped for air and called Justin's name.

"Justin. Did you get him? Is he dead?' I asked as Justin stood over his body.

He let off another shot in Abaddon's back before he turned to me and said it was over.

"Not yet." Maria said as we heard footsteps on the front porch.

Justin ran over and pulled me up to my feet as I told him about the door in the sunroom.

"Let's go then." he said as he held me up and Maria held up the rear.

We quickly made it in there and out the secret door into the backyard as shots ripped through the wall. Maria and Justin returned fire as we made our way across the yard back towards our car.

"A'Miracle." I said once I glanced over at the tree house and saw the door was open. "She is in there Justin. We have to go get her." I said to him as he changed directions and led us right over to the treehouse.

Justin propped me on the tree with Maria standing guard as he went up. As soon as he got to the top and we heard his footsteps, shots began to ring out. I staggered to my feet with my gun up as I yelled his name. I just knew he was dead when everything grew silent, but I was so wrong. Seconds later Adrain's body came soaring through the air as he fell to the ground.

"A'Miracle not there but he was and its blood all over the place. Where the fuck is my baby?" Justin asked as he climbed down, and I stomped Adrain in the face.

He laughed that inherited, evil chuckle as he held the wound in his belly then he pointed to the hill beside the property. We all looked up just as the nurse pulled A'Miracle across the hill as they were trailed by Abaddon. He was bloody from head to toe and staggering but the bastard was still alive. I couldn't believe my eyes as I stared that way and called his name.

"ADRIK! Let her go." I screamed out of my mind with rage as Abaddon stopped and turned around.

He smirked down the hill at me as I fired shots that missed him by at least a foot.

"You still haven't learned yet have you Jess. You can't beat me." he said as he laughed and then coughed up blood.

I wanted to just run up there and kill him, but I knew he's be gone before I made it halfway across the yard. That's why I decided to just use our leverage as I turned to Justin who was still beating Adrain.

"Bring him over here and hold him up. The bag too." I told Justin and he did just that.

He drug Adrian over in front of me and put him on his knees before he opened the bag and threw it to the ground.

"Give us our daughter or your favorite son is dead." Justin said enraged as I grabbed one of the books from the bag.

It had this big crest on the front and some words written in Russian. That let me know it was important, so I held it up over Adrain's head as Abaddon gasped.

"Give me my baby or your son dies and so will everyone else in your family. I have all the secrets, addresses, and phone numbers right here. GIVE ME A'MIRACLE!" I yelled as I saw Abaddon begin to sway.

He begged me to let his son go as he looked down at Adrian's bloody face and told him it would be alright. I showed him it wouldn't be as I put my gun to the back of his head.

"No, it won't unless you do what you are told. GIVE ME MY BABY!" I screamed as I squeezed on the trigger a little harder and Abaddon reached over to grab A'Miracle.

He looked down at her and then pulled her forward like he was about to let her go. He didn't get a chance to do that though before shots rang out all around us like fireworks on the fourth of July. The last thing I saw before darkness, my friend, found me was A'Miracle being drug over the hill.

Bitter Baby Daddy: When A Loser Can't Let Go

PREGNANT
By My Mother's
RAPIST
NIKI JILVONTAE

SINS
OF A MISFIT
NATIONAL BESTSELLING AUTHOR
NIKI JILVONTAE